The d
began
evade d
after h
But
side-b
directi

Trapped, the terrorist turned to confront Harry.

For one brief instant the two looked at each other. Harry remembered the terrorist, and the terrorist remembered Harry.

As if they were actors in a Western, the two men faced off, both with guns raised in their hands, knowing that in this duel one or the other, maybe both, would have to die.

The terrorist opened up just as Harry threw himself to the ground. . . .

The Dirty Harry series by Dane Hartman available from New English Library:

DUEL FOR CANNONS
DEATH ON THE DOCKS
THE LONG DEATH
THE MEXICO KILL
FAMILY SKELETONS
CITY OF BLOOD

CITY OF BLOOD

Dane Hartman

NEW ENGLISH LIBRARY

First published in the USA in 1982 by Warner Books Inc.

First NEL Paperback Edition January 1984

NEL Books are published by
New English Library,
Mill Road, Dunton Green,
Sevenoaks, Kent.
Editorial office: 47 Bedford Square, London WC1B 3DP

Made and printed in Great Britain by
Richard Clay (The Chaucer Press) Ltd,
Bungay, Suffolk

British Library C.I.P.

Hartman, Dane

City of blood.—(Dirty Harry; no. 6)
I. Title II. Series
813'.54[F] PS3558.A/

ISBN 0-450-05650-3

The Beginning

At four-thirty in the afternoon the Tocador Hotel is a quiet place. The street that adjoins it, in the Union Square area, is virtually devoid of traffic, so none of the residents of the hotel are obliged to suffer the rumble of passing cars or the occasional wail of a siren, signaling disaster of one sort or another.

As its name would indicate, the Tocador has a certain unpretentious Spanish ambience. You enter through filigree gates into a courtyard where ailanthus trees keep the unused and unusable fountain perpetually in shadow. There is a certain air of obsolescence about this place; the courtyard, with its cracked stone surface, and the lobby, with its chipped and broken tiles on the floor and the paint fading on its walls, all testify to the gentle ruin time has been responsible for.

The clerk who sat at the desk of the Tocador, with a registry larger than a Guttenberg Bible stretched open before him, was a man who had aged along with the hotel, growing a bit moldy himself. His skin seemed vaguely greenish and exuded a smell of faint decay that was probably the result of weeks without a shower.

The Tocador was largely a residential hotel. The people who lived there had been living there for years, cooking in the kitchens most of the apartments contained, which explained why no restaurant could be found in the establishment. The clerk knew the great majority of the residents; they were older than he and shambled rather than walked, relying on canes and walkers to get from the lobby's entrance to the elevators that were more cranky than the people who went up in them. It was always with some surprise that he greeted a guest who wished to be put up for only one or two nights. No guide book, save for the most thorough ones, even bothered mentioning the Tocador.

But the mere appearance of an unfamiliar face was not enough to startle the clerk, who passed most of his time on duty viewing soap operas and reruns of *The Million Dollar Movie* on the fuzzy black and white television mounted behind the counter. Most of those who sought temporary lodging in the Tocador were men who were down on their luck but who had yet to acknowledge the fact. Rates at the hotel edged on twenty dollars a day; it was generally more than the transients found they could afford, so they moved out before long, dragging suitcases that weighed half as much as they did.

This afternoon, however, as the big white clock in the lobby announced with a single chime that four-thirty had arrived, the clerk did have cause for surprise. More than surprise: utter astonishment.

For there, standing before him, were two of the most beautiful young women that he had ever had occasion to lay eyes on. Not that he had much basis for comparison. A widower, he did not get out much, but from what he had seen in magazines and on the television, which now was turned up way too loud to compensate for the clerk's failing hearing, these two were something else.

One was taller, leaner, a bit perkier in manner than the other. She wore a suede jacket edged with silver fox, and her long tan legs emerged from a velvet skirt. The other wore a cloche hat, a black leather jacket that was open to reveal a magenta silk skirt that was open in turn to reveal a slash of white skin, and black jodphur-like bloomers that extended to the upper perimeter of her ankles. Her toenails, peeking out of white sandals, he noticed were coated a bright lavender.

The taller one had black hair cut pageboy fashion so that her long and graceful neck was available for inspection. She seemed perpetually about to laugh, and her brown eyes were alive with the excitement of knowing something nobody else did. Her companion, by contrast, looked a bit quizzical, almost sullen, as though she were attempting to come to grips with some immense and troubling problem. But there was no question of the delicacy of her features, the sensuality of the lips, the flare of her nostrils, and the startlingly blue incandescence of her eyes.

The clerk rose to see what they wanted. He supposed they must be tourists who had gotten lost and were seeking directions. He felt years younger just to be in their presence and wished that he could persuade them to remain. But that, he realized, was unlikely; neither girl possessed any luggage, only their expensive handbags.

"What can I do for you?" he asked, clearing his throat, adjusting his glasses so that he could see them with greater clarity.

"We would like to register," the taller one said, almost giggling at this request. "That is unless you're full up."

Was their accent English? Maybe she was simply being affected. The clerk couldn't judge. But his astonishment was so great that he did not respond for a moment. Then he shook his head, as if to free himself from his daze.

"Full up? Oh no. Not at all." He turned the registry so that they could sign it.

"Is your luggage out in the car? I can bring it up to you."

The shorter, serious girl shook her head. "No, no luggage." Then she added gratuitously: "No car."

"No bags, no car," the clerk repeated wonderously. Then he remembered his responsibility: "That will be thirty-five dollars in advance. For a double?"

The taller girl who had just put her name down as Mary

Nold said that a double would be just fine and from her pocketbook uncoiled a roll of fifties. "You do have change, don't you?"

"Oh, of course, I do." The clerk stared stupidly at the display of money. He did not know what to make of it.

The other girl signed the name of Doris Paine. Both she and Mary gave their address as Palm Springs.

"Come quite a way," the clerk noted, inspecting what they had written.

"That's right," Doris said, seeming a bit annoyed. Obviously, she was not one for small talk. "Can we have the key to our room now?"

The clerk apologized. He wasn't thinking. "The key. Of course, the key." He produced one, a cumbersome thing with a brass ornament attached, upon which was inscribed the name of the hotel. "Room 358. It looks right out on the courtyard. I'm sure you'll be happy there."

"I'm sure we will," said Mary, taking it from him.

They turned from him and went to stand by the elevator.

The clerk called to them, suggesting that they might want to consider taking the stairs. The elevator could not be counted on, and the two girls looked to be fit enough to conquer two flights without trouble.

He kept his eyes on the stairs until their quick light footsteps no longer registered in his bad ears. Only then did the thought cross his mind that these two were prostitutes, that that was why they had so much money on them. But then he could not adjust the image he held of a prostitute (fading looks, a body gone to seed, an expression of indifference frozen on her face) and match it to these two lovely, seemingly uncorrupted, young women. And even if they were prostitutes, of the high-priced kind he had heard about and only rarely seen, why would they choose to do business in a hotel such as this where no potential john could be expected to have the kind of money that they would demand for their services?

The clerk, rather than continue to trouble his mind about these mysterious ladies, returned his attention to the soap opera that he had been following for years; he knew the characters in it better than he knew anyone in real life. His absorption in this televized drama was such that he failed to notice when another arrival appeared in the lobby, a gentleman this time.

He was certainly not one of the regulars but he proceeded directly to the stairs, and though he had never been to the Tocador before in his life, he nonetheless knew enough not to wait for the elevator to take him where he wanted to go.

There was nothing special to distinguish him, to cause you to remember him later. He was dressed simply in a raincoat and carried an umbrella, which must have meant that he'd left his home early in the morning when rain still threatened. In his other hand he held a satchel of some kind, one that from the nicks and scars on its surface looked as though it had been used for several years.

With the TV blaring so loudly, and with the clerk so deaf, this newcomer escaped attention altogether. He continued up the two flights of stairs to the third floor. It was now ten minutes before the hour of five.

At the door to Room 358 the man halted. For several moments he contented himself with just staring at the door as if he expected it to open without his having to knock. His eyes darted from one end of the dimly lit corridor to the other. He finally gave a light tap on the door.

It was Mary who answered. Her suede jacket removed, she sported a silk shirt, vermilion in color with ruffled sleeves of white damask. The shirt was tight enough to dramatize the contours of her small breasts where the man's gaze first fell. He smiled, then raised his eyes to meet her own.

"How are you?" she asked, returning his smile and stepping aside so that he could enter. "We didn't expect you so soon."

The man shut the door behind him and carefully placed his umbrella and his satchel in the closet on his immediate right.

"I started out as soon as I received your call." He looked around the room which, like the rest of the hotel, had an air of genteel shabbiness. The curtains and the furniture and most certainly the floral-patterned wallpaper appeared to be bleached by the sun which in this late autumn afternoon still shone brightly through the window. "Where's our mutual friend?" he asked.

"In the bathroom. She'll be right out. Say, Teddy, why did you want us to come here? This is such a weird, out-of-the-way place."

The man smiled again. "I like out-of-the-way places," he said. "I like different things." His eyes, concentrated on her body, were slightly bloodshot and inflamed.

"I know," Mary said, almost resignedly, "I know all about your different things." Noticing that Teddy had yet to take off his raincoat she now urged him to do so. "That is unless you're feeling in an especially modest mood this afternoon."

Not only did Teddy proceed to remove his raincoat but he also went about slipping off his shirt. But there was no haste in his disrobing, no, he was a meticulous, very neat man, compulsive. He made sure every article of clothing was put away in the closet.

"You don't waste any time," said Doris emerging from the bathroom.

"Aren't you going to say hello?" Teddy asked, sitting naked on the double bed. He did nothing to conceal his erection, his legs spread wide. But the expression on his face, far from intimating at excitement, was simply indifferent.

"Hello," Doris spat the greeting out.

"You don't sound pleased. And it's been such a long time, too."

Doris said nothing to this, but Mary felt compelled to defend her friend and said, "Don't mind her. She's had a hard day."

"Doris, come over here."

Doris complied, sashaying across the room to the bed.

Teddy reached his hands up and slowly drew the gold chain from around her neck. Then he slipped his hands beneath the sensuous fabric of the magenta shirt, separating it where it had not been buttoned in order to more fully reveal her breasts.

"Careful," Doris said, "I don't want you tearing it. I didn't bring anything else."

"Aren't I always?" Teddy was not looking at Doris; his eyes were fixed entirely on Mary who stood there, waiting her turn, neither expectant nor bored. She looked as interested in what he was doing to her friend as she might have been in a moderately amusing movie.

The shirt altogether undone, Doris, with a simple shrug sloughed it off.

"Magnificent!" pronounced Teddy, cradling her ample breasts with his hands. In doing this, he resembled someone testing heads of lettuce for their respective weight.

Surrendering one breast, he slid his free hand down under the bloomers. "Already wet, that's very nice," he said.

Although Doris was still determined to maintain a sullen, disinterested expression, her breathing had become more rapid.

"Now I want you to come around in back of me," he instructed Mary. "You know what to do."

And Mary did. She had done this, with Doris and with others like Doris, more times than she could count—or cared to.

Almost as an afterthought she shed the leather skirt, dropping it in a heap to the floor, and kicked off her pumps, leaving herself bare below the waist. She then climbed up onto the bed and encircled Teddy with her arms. Then, so as to give her hands the necessary freedom to operate, she disengaged and began to knead the swell of his stomach with the skill of a professional masseuse, gradually working her way down to his groin, practically duplicating what Teddy was doing to Doris. This had the effect of further arousing Teddy; his eyes rolled up toward the ceiling, exposing a generous portion of the whites, his breathing was harsh and rasping, and from time to time he arched when Mary's touch proved too exquisite, too liable to bring him to climax. Doris remained where she was, the bloomers drawn halfway down her thighs, her pubis hidden from Mary's view by Teddy's head. A loud sucking noise, the sound of air popping from the vaginal cavity, was accompanied by a deep moan that Doris released involuntarily. Her head seemed to sway and lurch against her chest as though she were incapable of keeping it upright. Her face was lost in a tangle of hair.

Mary drew both her legs around Teddy's waist, clasping him stalwartly, so much so that she succeeded in unbalancing him and pulling him down to the bed. Teddy didn't seem to mind about this, and brought Doris down to join them.

And so as the sun dipped beneath the horizon, unleashing a brilliant spattering of color across the west, the two lovely ladies and their male friend expertly passed the time.

And when, for all his vigor and an energy that was astonishing in a man who was probably past fifty years of age, Teddy had to call it quits, it was not at the expense of Doris or Mary. Spent, Teddy indicated that he wouldn't mind watching them entertain each other for a while. This was unlike Teddy, who had in the past resisted any sport that he could not take part in.

But Teddy was the boss, the man with the money, and the two young women were certainly willing to provide him with another several minutes of amusement. They were accomplices in a sense, one could play the other's body with virtuoso technique. Teddy could draw only so much pleasure from them because, for all his experience with them, he hadn't quite mastered them.

Doris assumed the more active role, maneuvering her smooth, sweat-slickened pale body over Mary's finely tanned one. Mary lowered her lips to between Doris' legs, teasing her friend with a tongue that seemed in emerging to have no end.

Doris allowed her eyes to close, mingling the ecstatic violence of sensation with fantasies in her dazzled mind.

Teddy, watching this spectacle, seemed alternately amused and mystified as though he couldn't quite fathom how he had been left out, forgotten completely. When he rose from the bed neither of the two women noticed his movement. Nor did they react at all when he slid open the closet and stooped down to open the satchel he'd brought with him. Nor did they pay any attention as he rummaged about inside this satchel, finally extracting from it exactly what he wanted.

Whether they were both groaning now because of the dizzying heights they had managed to bring each other to or because they were still approaching those heights and needed a bit more stimulation before they actually got there Teddy did not know, did not care.

Instead, simply because it was more convenient since she was now the one on top, Teddy raised the blade, razor-sharp and almost scimitar-like in length, and with one deft motion, brought it directly down on the back of Mary's exposed neck, grateful that her hair was cut short enough to provide him with such a clear target.

The air made a slight, almost inaudible whooshing sound as the blade progressed down, but the sound it made on impact was, to Teddy's ears, abrasively loud. The edge of the knife had, for a fraction of a second, met with resistance from the bone. But it was too slight to more than briefly interrupt the passage of the knife straight through so that it severed the jugular vein with something very much like surgical precision. And, because of the force that Teddy had invested in this blow, the knife did not stop when it had decapitated Mary but continued farther to a depth of nearly two inches in Doris' right thigh, which just happened to be in the way.

Doris had to scream for both of them because Mary never had the opportunity to utter a word. The pain must have been fierce but short-lived; Mary's eyes were still closed in passion, her ingenious tongue still protruding from her lips, moist with the juices from Doris' vagina. The blow had not only separated her head from her body but also had propelled it into space, hurtling it like a rocket in the direction of the window. It never quite got there, dropping down on the rug with a steady jet of blood still shooting out of the wound, like a flame from a turboprop engine.

The blood that Mary's headless body released mingled with the blood that bubbled up from the deep gash Teddy had incidentally carved in the flesh of Doris' thigh. It was hard to tell whose blood was whose. Teddy himself was soaked in blood, but he scarcely paid heed to it.

Doris was not so badly wounded, however, that she'd become immobilized. But there was no question she was shocked. In her eyes was horror compounded by disbelief. She sought to clamber off the bed, throwing her body onto the floor, whimpering. Her voice was strangled. After that first anguished scream of horror she could not get another out.

Teddy, were he not so fearful of her cries alerting people in neighboring rooms, might have enjoyed pursuing her about for a few minutes longer. But he realized that once begun, this enterprise would have to be completed with speed.

So, by simply placing his bare foot on the swell of her buttocks, pinning her hard against the rug, he prevented her from escaping. "No, no, no, no, don't," she mumbled, fitfully sobbing.

Teddy knelt down on her back. She was squirming desperately below him, but she seemed capable of doing nothing more than claw at the threads of the rug. But when Teddy placed the knife against her neck, prepared to saw through rather than duplicate the cleaner strike he'd employed on Mary, Doris half-turned, bucking, almost forcing Teddy off of her.

She managed to free one arm sufficiently so that she could use it against her assailant. With more skill than Teddy had given her credit for, she jabbed him in the left eye with her hand, making best use of her long sharp fingernails.

"Bitch! Fucking bitch!" Teddy said, his eye stinging like crazy, suddenly filled with pain. He reeled back, half-blinded, but still he kept her pinned to the ground.

And, more importantly, he still had control of the knife, which he used, only dimly aware of where it was he was striking. He slashed and slashed until he met with only enfeebled resistance. When he could adequately see what was happening he glimpsed a woman who, while still alive, was crisscrossed by dozens of cuts that yawned open to let out ever more blood from the imprisonment of veins and arteries.

Teddy returned to his original objective: the neck. The problem was that Doris was turning this way and that, moving so often, groaning no longer with pleasure but with the immensity of pain from twenty or thirty locations, that it was difficult for him to cut evenly and true. And by her very movement, she ended up cutting herself, slicing additional skin from under her Adam's apple as she strained to get out from under the knife's constant threat.

Teddy decided that enough was enough and by pressing his entire body weight against the knife he forced it far enough down her throat to extinguish her life. Then, mindless of the geyser of blood that sprayed his face, he continued on, cutting, sawing, carving until, with a final tearing of skin, Doris' head was removed from her splendid body.

The savagery concluded, Teddy still had a final bit of business to attend to. Namely, the hands. These he detached with little problem; there was no one to resist him now. Then scooping up the hands in the bottom sheet from the bed (for the top one was simply too messy to be of any use), he wrapped the four of them and deposited them in his accommodating satchel. Naturally, he would have to take the heads along; he hadn't cut them off just for the sheer hell of it, though in truth he had rather enjoyed the task. With his blade, he cut substantial parts of the curtains to provide temporary shelter for these heads; then they too were added to the gory contents of the satchel.

Now he had to go about the tedious business of washing up. He was confident enough to take a long shower, whistling a song as he soaped himself and cleaned the blood from his body. And though a great deal of blood had spattered on the closet door, none of it had penetrated, so his clothes were as clean and as fresh as he.

Only one thing remained to be done. From out of his satchel he extracted a can of gasoline. It was a big enough can and the gas inside plentiful enough so that Teddy could sprinkle the entire room and adjoining bathroom with it. He even made sure to douse the torsos of Doris and Mary who had not yet finished bleeding.

Then, just before he left the room, Teddy snapped open his lighter and pressed it close to the gas-saturated rug. A bright yellow flame shot out, touched the fibers of the rug, and instantly a blaze roared into the air, almost singeing Teddy's hair and eyebrows. But Teddy didn't mind. On the contrary, he was quite pleased. "Good-bye," he called, "Good-bye!"

With satchel in hand, Teddy let himself out. The satchel was heavier than before, but Teddy was a strong man, and his step was as light as a man who woke up one spring day to find himself in love.

Chapter One

"This is some piece of art this fucker put together," muttered Al Bressler who in his years as a lieutenant on the San Francisco Police Force had witnessed many such artworks, though seldom one so macabre.

You had the feeling that Lieutenant Bressler stood a bit in awe at the spectacle that greeted him and his entourage. Here, in the rubble of what had once been a rentable room, practically nothing remained that was whole or wasn't charred or consumed entirely by the fire. Firemen were busy extinguishing what was left of the blaze. Three of them had had to be taken to the hospital, suffering from smoke inhalation. For the fire, which had begun in Room 358, had spread down half the third floor corridor, forcing those trapped in their rooms to either leap to the ground or else risk losing their lives after the fire had taken their oxygen. Four elderly residents, too intimidated to make the jump despite the nets the firemen had out for them, had met their death this way. Another had attempted to escape by dashing through the flames. He had managed to make it to the stairway but had sustained such terrible third-degree burns that little hope was held for his survival.

That meant five deaths, not counting the two the fire had evidently been set to cover. Not much was left of those two, not much had been left of them even before the fire had started from what investigators could determine. No fire could be so devastating that it would obliterate absolutely all evidence of heads and hands. But there could be no doubt; the blackened forms that lay in the middle of the room had been deprived of heads and hands before the fire.

Sergeant Reineke, who stood directly behind Bressler, coughing from the noxious fumes in the air, had to see for himself. He went and looked, then ran to the door and out of it, searching for someplace he could throw up in solitude. No such place existed in the vicinity, so he vomited right there in the hallway, disgorging his insides on the scorched floor.

Bressler had more of a stomach for these things, but even he was disgusted.

"Carson," he said, turning to another detective who'd accompanied him, "any chance we're going to get anything out of this?"

Carson, who generally excelled at digging up evidence where others had failed, shook his head sadly. "The fire's done a pretty good job of wiping out just about anything we could use." He gestured to the ceiling, then to the walls. "Look, there's nothing here the fire hasn't touched. For Chrissakes, there's a good chance we'll never be able to identify these bodies. No hands, no fingerprints. No heads, no dental plates. Whoever did this wasn't just a maniac. He knew what he was doing. Though it sickens me thinking there's some jerk walking around out there with a couple of heads and a quartet of loose hands. Gives me the willies, you know what I mean."

Bressler knew exactly what he meant.

The investigators adjourned to the lobby; the smoke was too dense to linger in the room, and it was obvious they weren't going to accomplish much until the firemen had finished with their work.

The lobby was crowded with members of the press who, denied access to the third floor, occupied themselves shouting questions at the fire department's arson squad chief, who was being exceptionally unhelpful. The news photographers and the TV mobile-camera units, having nothing of great interest to capture on film, aimed their cameras at the lobby's interior. Flashbulbs popped continuously. The Tocador Hotel would be famous by the time the eleven o'clock news was over, but not in the way the hotel's management would have hoped.

"What's his name?" Bressler asked, looking at the hapless man who sat in the office that was located just off the lobby. The man was hard of hearing and cupped his ear, straining to hear. He was pale and trembling; possibly he expected to be accused of the barbarous crime that had just been committed or else blamed for allowing it to occur.

"Melvin Tessel. He's the day clerk. Only one on duty." The detective who had just provided this information seemed heartened to see Bressler; probably glad to be relieved of the responsibility for interrogating a man who seemed to be half-deaf.

Bressler pulled up a chair next to where the clerk was sitting and addressed him as he would a not terribly bright schoolboy. "Now, Mr. Tessel, you say that you never saw anyone who might have followed the two ladies—" he glanced down at the report he had in his hands—"Doris Paine and Mary Nold."

Melvin Tessel shook his head worriedly. "I'm sorry, sir, you see I was busy watching *As the World Turns,* and I had it turned way up loud because of my ears, you understand."

"I understand, Mr. Tessel," Bressler said impatiently. "And you never saw anyone suspicious leave?"

"No, sir. Somebody strange would have caught my eye, but I didn't see no one."

"And it was only when one of the residents, a Mr. Tully in Room 372, called down to complain of smoke that you became aware there was a fire on the third floor?"

Melvin Tessel nodded in the affirmative.

"That will be all, Mr. Tessel. Tomorrow some of my men will probably want to take a statement from you, but if between now and then you remember anything else, anything at all no matter how unimportant it may seem, get in touch with me immediately." He thrust his card into the clerk's hand.

Then he strode out into the crowded lobby, refusing to speak to the reporters who badgered him for a comment. "I'll have something for you in the morning," he asserted, hoping that would satisfy them.

Actually, Bressler did not know what he'd have in the morning. It did not surprise him that a preliminary check with the authorities in Palm Springs had not yielded anything substantive regarding the identities of Misses Paine and Nold. No such names were listed in the telephone directory, and the poor bureaucrat who had been roused from bed and sent to study the municipal records and tax and electoral rolls could find nothing either.

It did not surprise Bressler; he'd assumed from the outset that the names were fraudulent. The girls could have come from anywhere in the country.

The case promised to be nothing but ugly and sordid and, worst of all, futile. The best forensic pathologist in the world was not going to find any useful leads from the charred, headless, handless remains he was saddled with. Unless the psychopath who was responsible for this butchery had committed similar crimes in the past or intended to repeat himself in the future, they might never solve the murders at all.

When such cases came his way Bressler invariably chose the same person to investigate them. A man whom he felt was absolutely appropriate for something like this: Inspector #71, Harry Callahan.

Harry didn't need to be told. He had an instinct about these things. As soon as he heard the news of what had happened at the Tocador Hotel he resigned himself to being assigned to the investigation. The more pitfalls a case held for a detective the more likely it was that Bressler would pick him in the hope that he would fuck up, and fuck up so catastrophically that he could be busted down to traffic cop. Harry had fucked up in the past, occasionally it was unavoidable, but generally he'd avoided the more unspeakable punishments that Bressler had in mind for him.

He had no sooner entered the Homicide Department, on the seventh floor of the Justice Building, than he was informed that Bressler was waiting to see him. It was ten minutes of nine in the morning, a day which up to now had shown no sign of ever clearing up enough to let the sun shine through. The murkiness of the atmosphere was reflected in Harry's face.

"You're going to burn out before your time, Harry," Bressler said, taking a good look at him.

"It's possible it's already happened," Harry wearily conceded.

"You know what they say about burning your candles at both ends."

"Speaking of burning, is this about the Tocador?"

"Yes, this is about the Tocador. You got a feel for this business, Harry." Sarcasm lay heavy in his voice.

Bressler raised his eyes to the clock on the wall. "In exactly one hour I am going to hold a news conference. The mayor will be there. And what I will say to the members of the press is that we will have the murders solved by the end of the month, that we have some significant leads, and that right now we have men out on the streets, watching for anyone who might be attempting to dispose of evidence of the crime." He regarded Harry almost sorrowfully. "In fact, only the last part is true. The rest of it is bullshit. There is, however, a pressing need to make an arrest in this. It would be one thing if you got two hookers stiffed. That's stuff for the *National Enquirer*.

Nobody worries. But what we have here is five additional stiffs, elderly residents of the damn hotel, respectable people eking out a living from Social Security checks."

He lifted a folder off his desk and held it up as though it were a trophy he'd just won. "What we got here is the Mission Street Knifer."

"What's he got to do with this?"

"We went through our records, ran everything through our computers, this is what we came up with, the only known murderer-mutilator we got actively running around town."

"But his victims are usually derelicts, winos. From what I can recall he's never gone in for women, never beheaded anybody."

Bressler did not seem disconcerted by this. He had expected Harry to raise the point. "What you're saying is on the one hand, we have a middle-class, maybe upper-class, mutilator who goes in big for chopping hands and heads off. Now our lower-class mutilator, he goes in big for hearts and genitals. A difference in class, and I suppose you'd say a difference in anatomical preference. People don't worry about your lower-class mutilator, no sex appeal to offing winos and junkies nodded out by the tracks. Pretty girls aren't likely to be his victims. Well, suppose our demented friend just decided to confuse the issue, change his M.O.?"

"I don't buy it," Harry said simply. "There are two different people involved."

Bressler sighed. As much as he wished he could disagree with Harry he recognized that only by a great deal of tortured reasoning could one arrive at the conclusion that the Mission Street Knifer was the same man as the one who had struck at the Tocador.

"Yeah, well, to tell you the truth, I don't buy it either. But you're going to find me the Mission Street Knifer anyhow because that's the only option I've got right now. Otherwise what do I have? Two stiffs, no prints, no dental plates, fake I.D.s. And no murder weapon, no witnesses, no nothing.

About all we've really got is some shreds of clothing the stiffs were wearing. People expect action, I'm going to give them action."

This sounded like sheer madness to Harry. "You've already got half a dozen men on the Knifer, Collins and Bonfiglio, what good is adding me going to do?"

"Just bring me the Knifer, Harry. Let me worry about the assignments." Bressler stepped to the door, opened it, and called out, "Would you show Officer Owens in please?"

What was this about? Harry sat gloomily, waiting to see who this Owens was and what part Bressler intended him to play in this affair. He doubted very much he'd care for it, no matter what it was.

Drake Owens looked like an actor, not a lead actor, not somebody whose name you'd see up on a marquee, but more like a character actor, the handsome, perennially boyish type who's always holding his hat in his hands in Westerns, saying, "Yes ma'am," almost apologetically because he is so attractive to women. He was slender, of solid build but not strapping. His hair was an unruly mop of dirty blondness, his eyes were as blue as San Francisco Bay on the sunniest of days. He gave Harry a polite, almost sheepish smile as if to say, I don't know what I'm doing here either, don't blame me for any of this.

"Harry, Drake Owens."

"Pleased to meet you, I've heard a great deal about you," Owens said.

"Not much of it good, I suppose."

"You said it, not me," Bressler interjected.

"Oh, I don't know about that," said Owens, whose voice was as smooth and calming as his appearance. "I've seen you at the shooting range. I've watched what you can do with a .44."

"I'd like to see what he could do with a mind," Bressler said, apparently incapable of resisting the dig. "Not that he doesn't have one understand, it's just that he seems only occasionally inclined to use it. Stay, Harry, I'm not finished."

So as not to allow Harry a chance to argue he continued, "Officer Owens will be your partner on this case. That is, he will aid you in capturing the Mission Street Knifer."

"Do you know what has happened to my partners?" Harry was speaking to Owens now, hoping to discourage him from undertaking this assignment.

Owens matter-of-factly answered: "Gerrard Fanducci, deceased. Deitzick, wounded. Gonsales, wounded. Smith, deceased. DiGeorgio, wounded. Moore, deceased."

Harry regarded him with astonishment. Not only had he known it all, but he'd gotten the names, the order, and their fates precisely. "And you still want to work with me?"

"I try not to go by precedent. Human beings would never have evolved if they had relied on precedent alone."

"Shit," Harry muttered, shaking his head. It wasn't that he objected to what Owens had said or the conviction with which he had said it. Rather it was the feeling that he was being burdened with the responsibility for another man's life, that he'd spend as much time protecting Owens from harm as he would running down the Knifer, Mission Street or Tocador, whichever came first.

"If it doesn't work out after a few weeks you can pull me off the case," Owens said, eager to allay Harry's fears.

"There is a special reason I am assigning Owens to you, Harry," Bressler said. "Owens is the best decoy we have on this force. It may surprise you to learn that in his past life Drake Owens was a star of TV and movies."

Owens demurred. "Sir, if I may, not exactly a star. But I did a lot of work in many forgettable films when I was living in L.A."

This man was full of surprises. "And you quit Hollywood to become a cop in San Francisco? You're more insane than I thought."

Owens laughed. Bressler only smiled. Bressler was the sort who never got beyond smiling, didn't want to give too much away.

"Well, I didn't think I was accomplishing very much being a bad actor in worse films. I decided to employ my talent in another direction is all."

"It's your life."

Or it was before he volunteered for duty with Harry Callahan.

Chapter Two

William Maxim Davis took the most stringent precautions in even the most routine of tasks. His houses in the bay area, and the two he owned and a third he leased in town for business purposes, were guarded by a private security agency that supplemented its contingent of armed watchmen and Belgian shepherds, specially trained to leap instantly for a man's throat if given a signal, with the most advanced electronic sensors and alarm equipment.

The times Davis left his office near Jackson Square were shifted constantly, the routes he took to and from work also varied so that no one could successfully predict his movements and plan his assassination.

The limousine that Davis rode in cost him almost a quarter of a million dollars. It was an extraordinary vehicle, not only because of the luxuries that it offered—the television and the telephone that connected him to his office or to any one of his branch offices around the world and the well-stocked refrigerator and the ample space in back—but because of the safety devices that had been installed in it.

The glass was naturally bulletproof. The tires were resilient enough to take several bullets before giving way, and in any case, the limousine could still navigate at a sufficiently high speed even when all four tires were punctured. The gas tank occupied a position underneath the seat in the interior of the car so that no one could ignite it from the outside. (This did make it a cumbersome chore to replenish the gas, but like the older-model Mercedes, this tank held an enormous amount of fuel, and in any case, replenishing it was the sort of thing the chauffeurs were paid for.) The partition, between front and back, was remarkably strong; no bullet of any caliber could pass through it.

But the *pièce de résistance* in this elaborate system of defense was to be found under the seat next to where the chauffeur sat. In the likelihood that a terrorist could gain entrance to the vehicle, and threaten the driver, a final, and fatal, recourse was available.

A small toggle switch, within easy reach, could be pulled which would trigger a specially designed shotgun that was positioned underneath the cushion; it would then discharge upward, in rapid succession, three pellets into the ass and through the body of the unsuspecting terrorist. This would presumably have the effect of neutralizing any threat immediately.

Though assurances were given to all the chauffeurs that the pellets would continue through the roof if they exited from the body, Davis wasn't absolutely certain that they too wouldn't be injured in the blast. But he didn't care to warn them of this. It would, he believed, only disquiet them and make them more reluctant to resort to the use of the shotgun in the event of an emergency.

As befitted his position as the chairman of the board of Cavanaugh-Sterling, Davis was an imposing figure, forty-three years of age, with sandy hair turning gray about the edges and a face that seemed incapable of ever expressing passion, amusement, or joy. There had been no time for passion, amusement, or joy since Davis had begun his climb to the top of Cavanaugh-Sterling, a multinational corporation that had begun as a drugstore chain and branched out so promiscuously that it now owned moving lines, marinas, movie theaters, a cable TV network, granaries in the Midwest, shrimp fisheries in the South, a microchip factory in the North, and an aircraft company in the Northwest.

With Davis today was the diminutive, very dapper Mr. Hiroshi Asabuka, the production head of Cavanaugh-Sterling's Tokyo division. Asabuka loved jazz, baseball, and McDonald's hamburgers; in fact, he revelled in everything American. He admired Davis, believing that he was the forerunner of a new breed of American entrepreneur who would fundamentally restore the ailing economy and, not so incidentally, the uncertain political landscape.

The two, shadowed by the usual assortment of security guards, and accompanied by aides to Davis, who were all called vice presidents, regardless of how little power they actually wielded, were emerging from Cavanaugh-Sterling Headquarters, a gleaming new tower that was sheathed in glass tinted aquamarine.

Davis was a man who would look in both directions before crossing a one-way street; he was that cautious. Life represented a series of obstacles to be overcome. And the higher he rose in business the more obstacles there seemd to be. Which was not exactly what he'd expected when he started out.

Because of his substantial interests overseas, in Italy, the Middle East, and the Caribbean as well as in Japan, there was good reason for caution. Terrorists were launching attacks against businessmen with ever increasing frequency, and while these attacks had so far failed to happen in America, Davis, and his counterparts who managed other corporations, believed it only a matter of time before they, too, were targets of extremists.

But it is impossible for a man to concentrate entirely on matters of security—especially when that man's mind is filled with thoughts of mergers, SEC proceedings, and pretax profits. And, in any case, the private agency that Cavanaugh-

Sterling had authorized to protect its chief executive was supposed to concern itself with such things.

No one, however, was prepared for an outright assault on this rainy October afternoon. Jackson Square just didn't seem appropriate for something so bold and violent.

It was possible that the intended victim was not Davis but rather Asabuka, who was a notorious right wing fanatic in his own country, ever ready to chastise the Japanese citizenry for not doing enough to forestall the spread of world communism. Whomever was supposed to be assassinated was apparently never going to be clear simply because the assailants, who'd elected a rooftop to do their shooting from, opened up on everyone in sight.

The building that the gunmen had taken positions on faced Cavanaugh-Sterling Headquarters; it was a forgettable specimen of architecture that might have housed a welfare hotel or a bleak municipal office.

The rattle of gunfire at first seemed so far-off that Davis believed it a series of backfires from traffic on one of the neighboring streets. It was only when the guard in back of him lurched to the right, a small pink hole staining his white shirt, that Davis realized what was happening.

But by then another guard had thrown himself on Davis, sending him toppling down on the cold marble steps that descended from the Cavanaugh-Sterling building. Another man did the same to Asabuka, causing the small man's head to bang against the step, an injury much easier to recover from than a bullet wound.

But the assassins on the rooftop had the advantage not only of surprise but also of a commanding location. They could—and did—fire at will, scattering a hail of bullets along the steps, riddling three of the guards, two who now lay lifeless, draped over Asabuka and Davis and one of Davis' vice presidents.

More unpleasant than being in danger of his life, in Davis'

view, was lying helplessly on the steps while his bodyguard's blood leaked steadily onto his back and then began running down his face.

Only the Japanese seemed unconcerned; actually, he looked a bit entertained as though this were a Wild West show he'd somehow stumbled into. That he might meet his end any moment now was a fact that had yet to register in his mind.

One of the vice presidents, injured in an arm which hung limply at his side, a bloody swath of sinew where his shoulder ought to be, decided to climb back up the steps into the safety of the building. Groaning, he scrambled quickly and made it to the revolving door, perhaps thinking that his effort had paid off, only to discover that his progress had not gone unnoticed by the men on the rooftop. They busied themselves, almost in a sporting manner, emptying much of their clips into his back, causing blood to erupt in a dozen places. In this red shower the vice president promptly ended his career at Cavanaugh-Sterling. All things considered, he would have preferred a pink slip.

By this time, of course, witnesses inside the Cavanaugh-Sterling complex had caught on to what was happening and several phone calls had been made to the police.

Sirens could now be heard, signalling their impending arrival, but while the gunmen must have taken note of this they did not relent. On the contrary, they increased the intensity of their fusillade.

Davis realized that the assassins would have undoubtedly provided for an escape route, over onto another rooftop or through a secret passageway in the building whose rooftop they now occupied, and that it was likely the police had not been informed of what sort of opposition they should expect. A SWAT team would be necessary, not a contingent of patrol cops.

Despite the danger, Davis was only marginally interested in how this confrontation would turn out. For one thing, he was convinced, with that certainty that had gotten him this far, that he would survive. For another, he had business to attend to, a dinner date with a pretty woman, and this assault was going to make him very late. What's more, he would have to go back to his office and change; he was unaccustomed to having blood all over his Brooks Brothers suit.

At last a police cruiser came into view, stopping just past the intersection, out of the line of fire. Two patrolmen appeared, guns raised, but no sooner had they emerged from their car than they recognized how little good they could do in a situation like this. They returned to the safety of the cruiser and radioed in for more substantial backup.

In the meantime, other cruisers pulled up along with the occasional unmarked car. Inside one of these unmarked cars, with a license plate that began with the letter Z—the telltale sign of police proprietorship throughout the country—sat Harry Callahan and his newest partner, Drake Owens.

It was Owens' decision to accompany Harry; whoever the snipers were they were clearly not the Mission Street Knifer and that was all, theoretically, that Owens was responsible for. However, he had insisted, partially, Harry suspected, because he wished to prove that he had a talent for doing something other than playing bit parts in Grade B movies.

Though his colleagues were seemingly content to sit and wait until reinforcements and additional firepower arrived, Harry refused to wait along with them. Followed by Owens, he headed around the block, thinking that there might be access to the rear of the building where the gunmen were.

But their hopes proved short-lived. For there was another building, a bank crowned by a neoclassical cupola, that stood in the way. Nor was there any alleyway by which they could gain the entrance they sought. There was no doubt that the only way to get into the building was directly through the front door; to try and do that meant exposing oneself to the steady barrage the gunmen continued to lay down.

"What do we do now?" Owens asked, in some way relieved that their options had been foreclosed, that they, too, would have to wait for a SWAT team. This seemed to demand a military-scale operation in any case if they were to dislodge the men from the rooftop.

"What we do now is go in by the front," Harry said, none too pleased by the prospect himself.

"We could get killed doing that," Owens pointed out.

"We certainly could." The unspoken offer was there in his voice; if Owens wished to back out Harry would pose no objection.

But Owens had no intention of doing so. He just silently prayed that Harry knew what he was doing.

Harry had an idea but didn't exactly know. He motioned to Owens, and they made another circle of the block, this time from the other side. Observing the physical configuration of the street they looked down, the manner in which the buildings were arrayed, the way in which cornices and buttresses and gutter pipes protruded, and the present position of the shadows along the surface of the adjoining sidewalk, he told Owens, "Seems to me if we stick close to the buildings, staying within the border defined by the shadows, we have a fairly good chance to avoid being spotted."

Across the street, pinned down on the great white marble steps, Davis and members of his entourage, alive and dead and in between, were clustered cheek and jowl with one another. Blood drained down the steps in rivulets, forming small pools in the crevices and sags that the weather and the passage of thousands of feet had produced over time.

Otherwise, the street was deserted, pedestrian traffic having instantly come to a halt when the firing broke out. One man, unwittingly caught in the shooting, lay sprawled out in the middle of the street, his trenchcoat stained with blood, his umbrella thrown to the side; but he was still alive, wiggling slowly, hopelessely, in the direction of the intersection. No one could get help to him any more than they could get help to the people on the steps.

A gray limousine parked in front of Cavanaugh-Sterling Headquarters (a rented limo, not Davis' special) sustained some of the injuries intended for its prospective passengers. Windows would pop loudly as the bullets impacted. A series of jagged holes appeared across its chassis. It occurred to Harry that the gunmen were not simply failing to hit their human targets but were having some sport as well, riddling the limousine, perhaps to express their ideological antipathy to such extravagant means of transportation.

But the fate of this limousine (very likely the scrap heap) was of no concern to Harry. He now directed Owens, proceeding quickly, maneuvering as close as he could alongside the structures fronting the street. The din at this point was quite furious, what with the incessent gunfire and the mad cacophony of sirens that signalled the approach of yet more cruisers, ambulances, rescue trucks, and police vans.

So long as no gunman peered down from the edge of the rooftop Harry and Owens could consider themselves safe. But their luck stretched only so far. As they came near to their objective the sidewalk exploded just behind Harry and immediately in front of Owens, sending up a cloud of dust and cement fragments that began raining down on them.

Because there was no sense in returning the fire—they could barely expect to hit their antagonists from their earthbound position—they ran, zigzagging, no longer worried about the protection of the shadows since they'd already been seen.

Their tactics did not go unrewarded. The bullets that carved out great swaths of the sidewalk failed to hit them. Moreover, the terrorists could not concentrate entirely on the two men directly below them if they were to keep the men across the street from escaping.

Breathing hard, their lungs straining from the exertion, Harry and Owens found themselves at the dull green door that led into the building they wanted. Over the door a sign read "Animal Shelter League," but by the looks of this sign, and the drab facade itself, the Animal Shelter League people and their adopted pets had moved out long ago, leaving behind empty rooms and lots of dust.

The door was locked but the lock was not strong enough to resist the strength of a .44 round which easily mangled the shabby armor.

In the event that one of the gunmen was waiting in ambush, Harry kicked open the door and stood back. Owens faced him, flush against the opposite jamb.

Harry then dived into a hallway that hadn't seen light, natural or artificial, for several years. Owens duplicated his maneuver, his .356 Magnum extended in his hands.

No opposition presented itself, only a faint smell of must and decay reached their nostrils as they crouched warily, trying to make out what awaited them in the profound darkness.

Silently, the two men started to move, using their hands like the blind to guide themselves down the hallway. Within half a minute they had fully explored the entirety of the groundfloor in this clumsy manner, and yet had failed to locate any means of ascending higher in the building. Harry risked employing his lighter, sending a small flame into the air that was sufficient to reveal a door to a freight elevator and by its side the button that apparently could control it.

Owens pushed. They waited, at first hearing nothing but the muffled rattle of gunfire in the street and the more distant shriek of sirens.

Then, from high up in the shaft came the groaning, tortured sound of cables and obsolescent machinery. The antiquated elevator began its grudging descent but there was, of course, no way of telling whether anyone was descending with it.

The elevator's groaning became louder and then ceased altogether as it came to a rest. Nobody got out. The elevator was unoccupied, and the two of them entered.

The buttons on the elevator's interior wall indicated that

twelve was as high as they were going to go; presumably, from that floor one could gain access to the roof.

Before they commenced their treacherous climb, Harry surveyed their confined circumstances, determining with his eye that the roof of the elevator could be made to open. It would be a mistake—and very likely a fatal one—to remain imprisoned by the elevator, especially as it attained the twelfth floor. It was obvious that the snipers would be awaiting their arrival.

To avoid this unhappy prospect, Harry decided it best if they rode on top of the elevator. Owens, being the lighter of the two, supported himself on Harry's shoulders and by exerting all the strength in his arms forced the door open. Then he grasped hold of the sharp rusted surface of the roof and pulled himself up.

Harry now depressed the button designated 12, and while the elevator responded, beginning to move slowly, Owens helped him up and out onto the roof. It was a tricky maneuver, one that a mastery of Alpine mountaineering would have helped. But the possibility of a quick violent end is powerful incentive; mothers have been known to lift cars weighing tons when their children have been trapped beneath them. Harry could conquer the canvas-lined wall of a freight elevator.

Both men now safely on the roof of the elevator, they stretched out, hugging the surface. No telling how much space would be available between the cable supports and the top of the elevator. It wouldn't be of much use to survive a terrorist's attack, only to be mashed by indifferent machinery.

Certainly when viewed from their angle, the thicket of cables looked intimidating. It was possible to believe that the elevator wouldn't stop, that it would keep right on going, allowing Harry and his partner to be sucked into the fearsome motor that kept the whole thing in motion.

The all-too-familiar staccato of gunfire reached their ears as they came closer to their destination. Gradually, the churning wheels about which the cables continued to revolve slowed and creaked to a halt. The twelfth floor.

Somebody was opening the door but only enough to permit him to spray the elevator's interior with a succession of rounds that tore apart the canvas, echoed off the metal walls underneath, and sent up a poisonous smell of cordite into the air.

The gunman who wielded a Belgian FN MAG machine gun, the kind mercenaries fighting in Rhodesia used, stepped into the elevator, clearly astonished that he hadn't hit anyone and that there was no one to hit in the first place.

Before he could glance upward and see that the door to the roof of the cabin was open, Harry fired his .44, striking the man in the chest. The gunman was flung way back, slamming against the wall he had just ripped up with his FN. His eyes were wide with shock and surprise that his strategy had so obviously and catastrophically come to an end. He slumped down on the floor and loosened a short burst from his FN, a futile gesture but one that he probably found as consoling as a priest's last rites.

Harry quickly leaped down through the opening, expecting to have to contend with the deceased's equally murderous comrades, but they were either too busy wreaking havoc on the steps of the Cavanaugh-Sterling headquarters or else operating on the premise that the problem coming up on the elevator had been eliminated.

Owens followed Harry down. Before they abandoned the elevator they confiscated the FN, seeing as how the dead man was not going to be using it where he was headed. It was difficult to determine the nationality of the terrorist; he was swarthy, though that could have been merely because he liked the great outdoors, and he sported a bushy beard that pretty much dominated his face. They had no time to search him or note any other distinguishing attributes.

Opening the door that entered onto a hallway that looked no different in the darkness than the one on the ground floor, they instinctively turned in the direction of the firing. A small speck of light to their left aided their search.

As they proceeded toward this light, they realized that it was leaking in from a door that presumably yielded onto the roof.

"From here on in we continue firing," Harry said. "Take out as many as you can with this thing." He handed Owens the FN.

Owens was not expecting this. "Don't you want it?"

"You don't know how to use it? Is that what you mean?"

Owens shook his head; he'd had experience with machine guns before, when he served in Vietnam for a year's tour, but he had just naturally assumed Harry would prefer the benefit of its rapid firing.

Not so. Harry held out his .44. "You believe something gives you luck, you go with it."

"You're the boss."

Owens had never been on a parachute jump, all his training and battling had kept him to the ground, but he imagined that this was what it felt like when for the first time you were standing at the door about to leap from a plane twenty thousand feet in the air, stomach lurching, heart beating crazily, wondering whether your chute would open.

It was a different sort of door now and a different sort of jump. Only the danger was far greater.

Harry stood, his hand gripping the handle, waiting as if for some signal. It would have to come from his own mind, from his instincts, because with no window to see what was happening outside, they would never have any means of knowing which moment to launch their assault was the most propitious.

As soon as the door flew open, Harry flung himself on the asphalt surface of the roof. Owens followed his example, and when they had flattened themselves out, they opened fire.

Across from them, crouched behind a low-lying protective wall that extended about the entire perimeter of the roof, were two snipers, both of whom were maintaining their barrage on the street. All that could be seen of them were their backs, their shoulders hunched high enough to blot out almost all view of their heads. Their bodies shuddered repeatedly with the recoil from their guns, but clearly they were accustomed to it.

Because of the time element involved and the necessity of protecting themselves, neither of the guns discharged by Owens and Callahan did as much damage as they should have were they properly sighted. But they did enough.

One of the snipers sustained a blast of the FN in his upper shoulder, which forced his weapon from his hand. Another gouged out a huge chunk of the brick wall, propelling it upward so that it hit this same gunman in his gut, further debilitating him.

The second narrowly escaped Harry's fire, but that was only because he had unexpectedly shifted position. Turning to see where this attack was coming from, he fared much worse, for the round that Harry now fired made a mess of his stomach and sent him toppling over to the street. His scream persisted for as long as it took him to plummet to the ground: not long.

The surviving sniper had no opportunity in which to consolidate himself, for Owens had him correctly targeted by this point and, without a moment's hesitation, loosened another burst from the Belgian machine gun. Though this gunman did not make his exit from the world so dramatically as his companion had, his death was every bit as thorough. He crashed to the asphalt and immediately began to pour blood onto its dull, sunbaked topography.

It was only then that Owens allowed himself the luxury of standing erect in order to better survey the scene. Twelve floors below there was shouting as people gradually understood that the danger had passed, that they could move out into the street again without sustaining a gunshot wound.

But it was not the shouting that Harry heard but something else, a softer, almost inaudible sound from their left. He reached out, grabbing hold of Owens' ankle and virtually threw him down.

Owens reacted with annoyance. "What did you do that for?"

Harry signalled him to be silent. "Over there," he whispered, "there's another one still alive."

Owens looked to where Harry was pointing but all he could see was the protrusion of an immense gray cooling unit that rested on pontoons and beyond that what looked like it might be a water tank of some kind. He noticed nothing unusual nor did he hear what it was that had Harry so alarmed.

But Owens was certainly not about to lose faith in Harry now. If Harry said there was someone there, why then he believed him.

Once Harry'd advised Owens to stay put, he began to crawl slowly in the direction of the cooling unit. He surmised that the fourth assailant, aware that his companions had been killed, had decided to break off the engagement and was now hiding, hoping to avoid discovery, at least long enough for him to make good his escape. And the route of that escape was evident enough to Harry. Denied the use of the elevator, the gunman would have to resort to the adjacent rooftops that were about as high off the ground as this one, meaning he wouldn't have to chance limb-breaking jumps as he ran. No doubt considerable reconnaissance had gone into this operation before it was undertaken.

Whether Harry's antagonist panicked or whether he actually thought he had a decent chance of hitting him, Harry didn't know, but all at once the asphalt in front of Harry spewed into the air as a succession of rounds tore into it.

Instantly, Harry rolled away. And before he could return the fire, Owens was doing so for him, spraying the cooling system, puncturing a trail of holes into the weather-beaten metal. Water bubbled out of the ruptured ducts, splashing down onto the roof with a roar that made it sound like a small Niagara.

Though he hadn't hit Harry's assailant, Owens had succeeded in driving him from his shelter. He could now be seen bolting in the direction of the next rooftop. Owens could barely make out his form and was in no position to hit him, not with the water tank and cooling unit in his way.

Harry, spitting out the asphalt dust that had gotten in his mouth and rubbing his eyes free of the same, started after him, oblivious of the water that cascaded down on him.

The escaping gunman was agile, that much was obvious, leapfrogging over the retaining wall, momentarily disappearing from sight until he picked himself up and began his scramble across the contiguous roof.

But in mid-motion he wheeled about, firing his Yugoslav FAZ automatic, a cousin of the famous—some would say notorious—Soviet AK machine gun. Lacking optimal balance, he failed to cause Harry injury, but he did force Harry down, which in turn allowed him the opportunity to put more distance between them.

The threatening afternoon skies, which had held off since morning, now unleashed a fierce downpour that did not even bother announcing itself with the formality of a drizzle. The rooftops were converted into instant pools, and the deluge of water made their surfaces more and more slippery until both Harry and the man he was chasing found the going increasingly difficult. And there was no question that either of them could proceed as fast, as nimbly, as they had before the skies broke.

They got onto their third rooftop, but only by a risky jump down one entire story. The impact was painful. Harry, coming down on his knees, had momentarily stumbled and fallen into a gathering, mud-clotted lake. After lifting himself to his feet with difficulty, he could no longer see the man.

He continued to the rooftop's edge and peered down. This was as far as one could go. Either the terrorist had leaped eleven floors, which was unlikely given his determination to extend his lifetime beyond this afternoon, or he had somehow found another way off the roof.

By further exploring the geography of this third roof, Harry discovered a door that gave access to the building itself. Cautiously, he proceeded down the steps that led into a brightly lit hall. But the terrorist hadn't decided to linger in hope of ambushing him. He had chosen more wisely and had simply vanished.

Chapter Three

Fresh cologne could not entirely eradicate the faint scent of blood, but otherwise there was nothing about William Davis' appearance or demeanor to suggest the ordeal that he had just undergone.

A small dressing room adjoined his office on the twenty-fifth, and highest, floor of Cavanaugh-Sterling Headquarters, and it was there that Davis had showered and changed while Harry and Owens waited for him.

Davis' office was elaborately paneled; the walls were of teak and rosewood, the furniture mahogany and fine ebony. The atmosphere was subtle, and, without the lights set discreetly into the walls, dark as a rainforest at night. Harry had expected a window vast and panoramic so that Davis' sense of power could be confirmed by the view. But there was no window, only paintings: a Rothko canvas, all browns and blacks, a dreary landscape of Edvard Munch, a depiction of grotesques that looked like a Bosch.

On his desk, which was so empty as to suggest that all of Davis' work had either been completed or consigned to others, there was one black push-button phone with three extensions and a framed photograph of a frail-looking woman whose hair was pulled back; she was pretty enough but wan, and her expression intimated at some great sadness. Harry, taking advantage of Davis' absence, regarded it closely. He guessed that the woman must be Davis' wife.

Unlike Davis, neither Harry nor Owens had enjoyed the opportunity to change, and they looked less like police officers than derelicts of the sort that were favored by the Mission Street Knifer: mud-spattered and bloody, their hair unkempt and dirt-ridden, their trousers ripped, bruises everywhere on their flesh. Until they'd displayed their badges to the security officials in the lobby, they had stood in danger of being arrested by their uniformed colleagues on charges of trespassing. Even then they were made to wipe their feet clean of mud lest they stain the expensive carpets that lined every corridor and smothered every office floor.

Davis, emerging from his dressing room, regarded them with some amusement. He took a seat behind his desk and spread out his hands on the blotter, taking hold of a pen and absently tapping it on the pointed ebony surface.

"I understand you were the two who neutralized the terrorists," he said, taking the initiative in the conversation although he was the one who was supposed to answer questions, not issue statements.

Harry, in no mood to be particularly deferential, no matter that the man before him was a self-made millionaire who wielded immense economic and, of course, political influence, cut him off. "Why do you think this attack was made? Do you believe you were the exclusive target?"

"Of course. You realize that this terrorist strike, because it was that, mark my words, was meant also to decimate much of Cavanaugh-Sterling's top leadership. And unhappily, two of my vice presidents were murdered."

There was nothing in his tone of voice, Harry noted, to indicate that Davis was suffering from their premature demise.

"I am grateful that my Japanese friend—"

"That would be Mr. Asabuka?" Owens said, consulting his hastily drawn-up notes.

"Correct. He sustained nothing more than a bruised scalp. But there are men to replace the men we lost."

"Your vice presidents?" Harry asked, wanting him to be precise.

"Yes."

"And what about your security men?"

Davis seemed to have forgotten about them. "Oh yes, naturally."

"Why would terrorists wish to carry out such a strike against you and others here at Cavanaugh-Sterling?"

"Because we are capitalists, we believe in free enterprise, and there are those elements, foreign and domestic, which oppose our investment policies, our expansion, accusing us of exploitation, the usual errant nonsense. . . ."

"Who do you believe these terrorists are exactly? Have you any idea where they might have come from?"

"I would assume they'd have to be imported. From Nicaragua, from San Salvador maybe. Possibly Cuba. Anywhere where revolutionaries can flourish. But what is an outrage is that such an attack could take place here in San Francisco. I am surprised and alarmed that the police would allow these people to operate freely."

"I don't know what you mean by that."

Davis held up his hand in an attempt to forestall any rebuttal.

"I want to make it clear that I am not implicating either of you two gentlemen. As far as I'm concerned you are the only ones to show any courage, any balls. Everyone else I noticed was paralyzed, rooted to the spot, waiting for God knows what, the National Guard, maybe hoping the Strategic Air Command would nuke the sons of bitches. Only you two seized the chance, risked your lives, and I want you to know that if I can do anything for you in the future, either of you, I would be happy to lend whatever assistance I can."

His phone rang. He excused himself, picking it up. "No, no,

I don't want to be disturbed now. I am not about to speak to the reporters. Tell them I have no statement."

He slammed the phone back down, stared hard at Harry and Owens as if to determine who they might be and why they were sitting here in his office. Then he allowed a smile, as cryptic as the one Leonardo gave to the Mona Lisa, to come to his lips. "Will that be all or is there anything else I can do for you?"

Harry rose, sensing that he was unlikely to acquire any useful responses from Davis so long as he remained on his own turf. He was too fully in command and confident of himself, showing no visible sign that he was ever in fear for his life. Being pinned down on the steps of his building, protected from death only because one of his loyal security men had permitted his body to be used as a receptacle for bullets intended for him, had failed to make any apparent impression. Accidentally burning his fingers with a match would probably have aggravated and disturbed him more. And his detached attitude in the face of the deaths of his corporate officers, not to mention his guards, struck Harry as very odd.

"No, I think that's all for now," he said politely. "We will probably have some more questions for you later. In the meantime, I suggest that you and your staff exercise extreme caution. There is every possibility that the terrorists, if that's what they are, might strike again."

"No problem. Cavanaugh-Sterling takes care of its own."

"If they take care of their own," Harry said to Owens once they had stepped out into the corridor, beyond Davis' hearing range, "they sure as hell haven't done a very good job of it so far."

"I don't like that guy," Owens offered. "Seems to me like a heartless bastard."

Harry gave his new partner a searching look. Then he smiled.

"You know, Drake, we might get along well after all."

The following morning, the *Chronicle,* in a banner headline that descended nearly halfway down the front page, declared woefully that San Francisco had become a "city of blood." A large photograph, taken as soon as the sniper firing had ceased by an intrepid newsman willing to put his life on the line for a Pulitzer, showed what the steps of Cavanaugh-Sterling Headquarters had looked like at four-thirty in the afternoon: bodies strewn haphazardly, patches of blood smearing the marble, figures dazedly pulling themselves erect, paramedics bearing stretchers as they rushed to the aid of the injured. . . . The accompanying story tied together, in not always believable fashion, the terrorist attack, the unsolved murders and fire that had occurred at the Tocador Hotel, and the spate of mutilations accredited to the so-called Mission Street Knifer.

That these three violent eruptions were probably unrelated (Bressler's statements to the press notwithstanding), that their only link was that they occurred within a short time of one another, made little difference to the reporter who wrote the news analysis.

Harry sat at a saloon called Ramble's, getting around to reading the paper finally by mid-afternoon, interested in seeing how distorted the account turned out. He was relieved to find that his name had been spelled right.

A bright October sun, again in the ascendancy following yesterday's severe drenching, streamed in through the big square window of the bar.

At half past three, precisely on schedule, Owens strolled into the bar and joined Harry.

"You're a hero," he said, indicating the paper that Harry now had turned to the sports section.

"Some hero," Harry muttered. He was more interested in the Phillies' chances of winning the pennant.

"What's wrong, you got something against the Astros?"

"Yeah, I don't like Houston. And I don't like artificial turf."

"Phillies have artificial turf," Owens pointed out.

"Have to forgive them then. You gotta forgive them for

being in Philadelphia in the first place. After that it's easy to forgive them anything."

Owens wasn't sure he followed the logic of this, decided not to pursue the subject, and ordered a Coors.

"What do you say to a home cooked meal, Harry?"

"Home cooked meal?" Harry sounded almost incredulous. A man used to fast-food joints, takeouts, sandwiches gobbled down between cases, a man for whom indigestion was practically a way of life, Harry would have regarded a good meal in a moderately priced restaurant with a certain awe, but a home cooked meal? That was approaching the miraculous.

"You a good cook?"

"I can barbeque up a burger or steak, that's about all. No, it's my wife, Mary Beth, she's the one who'll prepare the meal. I thought it'd be a nice opportunity. She is dying to meet you. I told her all about you."

"All about me?" Harry gave Owens a questioning look.

"Nothing embarrassing."

Harry nodded. "Well, so long as we're through by seven."

Seven was when they were obliged to begin their search for the Mission Street Knifer. At least they could do so on full stomachs.

"No problem. The only thing is we have to pick Mary Beth up at work. Why don't you come along? You might find it interesting to see what she does."

"Oh, what does she do?"

"Wardrobe consultant for a movie they're shooting here in the city. I might have gotten out of the movies, she never really did. It's kind of like an addiction. She got starstruck as a kid, never outgrew it."

"Were you the star?"

Owens smiled. "Something like that."

They were headed in Owens' car, one of the new K-Cars Chrysler had just brought out in hope of resuscitating the company, in the direction of Polk Street, where the day's shooting was going on. "One thing you might find interesting to note," Owens told Harry before they arrived, "is that the production company doing this film is a wholly owned subsidiary of Cavanaugh-Sterling. Global Film Company it's called."

"That so? The fucker pops up everywhere," Harry commented ruefully.

There was no doubt in Owens' mind that he was referring to William Maxim Davis.

"It's a long way from chairman of the board to a wardrobe consultant."

"Don't think I was implicating your wife. A job's a job. From what I hear breaking into movie work is a bitch."

"Unless you know somebody. It's all connections. That's what the business is, connections."

"That's what every business is, believe it."

Just ahead of them, not far from where Bush intersects with Polk, they beheld a line of awesomely large white vans, parked one after another, some filled with equipment, others the temporary residences of the cast and crew. There was just one parking space on the block, and Owens found it.

"When it comes to parking spaces," he explained, "I got this weird luck. Places people say are impossible to park, where you've got to drive around for hours before you give up and go to a garage, I find something right away. Don't ask me how I do it. Only problem is I think sometimes when I really need some luck, God'll say: 'Tough tittie, Drake, you exhausted your quota on parking spaces.' "

Harry found this amusing. Owens was so different from his previous partners—he was in fact unlike anyone on the force he'd ever met—that Harry didn't quite know what to make of him. His sense of humor, the casual manner he affected, his self-effacing quality which Harry assumed to be extremely rare in an actor, former or current, distinguished him from his colleagues and might well account for some predictable skepticism on their part. They would, as Harry had been tempted to do, consider him a dim prospect when it came to the demands of police work that was anything more than routine. But Owens had amply demonstrated his courage and competence yesterday afternoon, which was about all the convincing that Harry needed.

Only thing was, Harry found himself liking Owens. Bad enough to lose your partners, it was worse when those partners were friends as well.

They were walking past a place called Mom's Apple Grave, whose window displayed not just a baffling feast of exotic and colorful clothes but an open casket with an unhappy-looking skeleton resting inside it. Harry thought it a good thing that he did not believe in signs and omens, for open caskets with skeletons exhibited for public inspection certainly did not augur well for the future.

Half a block away, powerful klieg lights surrounded by a tangle of cords and cables brought more intense illumination to the immediate area than even the afternoon sun could hope to provide.

It was impossible from a distance to determine who was in command or, for that matter, who were the actors and who were the members of the crew. All that one could say for sure was that no shooting was going on. Instead people were running around in all directions, screaming orders at one another, evidently in hope that whatever scene they were in the middle of filming could be reshot without further delay.

At last the preparations seemed done with. A young woman with a megaphone ordained silence. A man, who scarcely looked thirty, with unruly brown hair and wearing a turtleneck and jeans, likewise bearing a megaphone, seated himself in a folding chair with his name on it and shouted, "OK, let's get on with it." He yelled for a woman named Martha.

"Martha is Martha Denby, the actress," Owens explained to Harry.

Harry thought he'd heard of her somewhere along the line or maybe caught a picture she was in.

Martha now emerged from a boutique, which had been expropriated at least for the duration of the afternoon, for whatever scene this was. She was an attractive but by no means glamorous woman, slender, almost frail, with refined features and auburn hair. At this moment she looked a bit pallid, perhaps from the ordeal of going through this same scene again and again and again, and yet appealingly vulnerable, too.

She was wearing a silk cardigan jacket to her waist and a pleated skirt, wine-red in color, that extended to her ankles. Whenever she shifted her position, the front of the jacket would part sufficiently to reveal a surprising portion of her breasts, but the glimpse would last for no longer than a moment or two, before she'd shift, drawing the jacket together again. The breeze that was blowing in from the bay was growing stiffer, and the poor girl looked like she might be cold.

"They were shooting this scene yesterday," Owens said. "They were shooting it the day before yesterday. If I didn't know this business I'd never figure out how a movie ever got made. Sometimes, of course, they don't."

"Where's your wife?"

Owens gestured to one of the large white vans parked across the street. "She's in there. Don't worry, she finishes at five even if they go on with this shit all night."

Looking admiringly at Martha Denby, Harry assured his partner that he did not expect to be bored.

The scene was a short one even if the director was never very happy with it. Martha would make her entrance from the boutique, then stand quite still, a bewildered expression on her face as though she could not decide where she was going. Before a destination occurred to her, a man suddenly materialized on her right. So quickly and silently did he approach her that Harry was rather surprised; not having realized that he was an actor because he was standing off to one side, indifferently observing the proceedings, Harry had assumed he was one of the crew. But he was obviously in the picture, and when he stepped up to Martha, the actress grimaced, a look of fierce displeasure on her face.

"She has had an affair with this man," Owens explained, "but she's broken it off, never wants to see this guy again. He's a real bastard. She had to get a court order to keep him away."

"This is the movie you're talking about?"

Owens laughed but quietly so as not to disrupt the silence on the set. "Martha's personal history is something else again, from what Mary Beth says, but no, this is just the plot of the movie."

Now the actor, a young man who looked as malevolent as the script called for, began to speak to Martha, though what he was saying was inaudible to Harry and Owens, and would, in any case, later be dubbed in in a sound studio. Nonetheless, it was clear that the man was attempting to persuade the girl to accompany him somewhere. At the same time, others began to move into the scene, an elderly couple, a mother with child in tow, a man in a business suit toting a briefcase. They were meant to be pedestrians, and they passed by the two leads, ignoring their argument which, given the more frequent and more exaggerated gestures they were making, seemed to grow increasingly heated. The man caught hold of the girl's wrist and tried forcibly to drag her with him. She resisted and in doing so offered the viewers on the set and presumably, if the scene survived the cutting room, those in the movie theaters, a generous and tantalizing view of her breasts, which considering how very slender and small-boned she was, were astonishingly ample. Then the man released her and, apparently despairing of convincing her, threw up his arms and began to walk away.

A cameraman now dollied his equipment behind him while another camera remained focused on Martha who looked stricken, her face ghostly white, her mouth taut. All at once, she broke down, tears streamed from her eyes. She wheeled about and screamed—and this time Harry and Owens could hear—"Come back, damn you, come back!"

But the man kept walking, refusing to listen to her. She chased after him, sobbing, entreating him to stop. The man was not going very fast, and she had little difficulty in catching up with him.

"Cut!" the director shouted, rising from his chair triumphantly. "That's a take. That's a goddamn take!" His face expressed his jubilation.

"Well, maybe you brought some luck with you, Harry," Owens said. "That was as perfect as they'll ever get it."

"That was some piece of acting," Harry marveled.

The actress, savoring the moment, was no longer crying. On the contrary, she was every bit as happy as the director, maybe more so, and with girlish enthusiasm, she hugged her co-star and kissed the director.

"She just started living with the male lead, so don't get any ideas," said Owens, noting the glint in Harry's eyes.

"No ideas," he replied somewhat irritably. "Tell me, what happens after this?"

"After this I'm not quite certain. The script's a big secret, even the leads don't know exactly. But I do know that the man you saw there, his name's Jim Corona by the way, well, Jim, he takes her to a room somewhere and fucks her. And—"

He stopped, suddenly looking across the street. A woman was making her way toward him. Mary Beth.

"And what?" Harry prodded him.

"Oh, and then he murders her."

"Shit, can't get away from it anywhere," Harry muttered.

Owens wasn't listening. He was too busy greeting his wife, embracing her, then introducing her to Harry.

Mary Beth Owens was a fair-haired woman, with a pleasing face that suggested Midwestern-Scandinavian stock, and a figure that while slightly on the plump side would still make a man happy. Taking Harry's hand, she smiled demurely, "Well, it's a pleasure finally to make your acquaintance."

"Finally?" Hadn't she only heard about him the day before?

"Oh yes, Drake's spoke of you often. All your adventures inside the department and out. You don't realize you're something of a celebrity."

"It's nice of you to say so." Harry neglected to add that his was the sort of celebrity that inspired people to think of killing him.

"Now, Inspector Callahan, tell me, have you any objections to roast beef?"

Harry had no objections to roast beef, nor to the salad or baked potatoes that accompanied it. It was an all-American dinner served in a no-nonsense fashion. Harry had the impression that Mary Beth was an eminently practical woman, equally efficient at home or at work.

The Owens' house was a renovated two-story, Victorian-influenced structure. Five or six years ago the neighborhood in which it was located, half a dozen blocks or so from the celebrated intersection of Haight and Ashbury, would have been considered a slum. But now, with creeping gentrification, characterized by boutiques and drinking places that favored plants, picture windows, pretentious names, and a tendency to sell great quantities of Perrier and quiche to their clientele, the last thing anyone would call this area was a slum.

"This house for us is like a boat to others," Owens said. "There's always more restoration to be done or something to be fixed."

"That's where most of my wages go," Mary Beth added. "Our next objective is to insulate the attic. We can't afford it until next month."

"Next month," Owens scoffed. "You're a hopeless optimist." He did not seem to appreciate the contradiction in that last phrase. "My wife has a five-year plan for everything," he added, gently mocking. "First the attic, then we build more bookcases in the living room. . . ."

"Then we have a baby," Mary Beth put in, smiling mischievously. "In that order."

Owens laughed. "See if the City of San Francisco gives me a raise. Or if Global gives you one."

"The only way I'm going to keep working for Global is if I go to L.A. You know what I think of L.A. I wouldn't want my child conceived there, let alone born and raised there."

"Well," Owens said in the manner of a man who has repeated himself many times over, "money is money. And Global does pay well. Maybe there'll be more work for you in San Francisco. Who knows, maybe you'll find a job with another production company."

Mary Beth shrugged, evidently not anxious to continue discussing this subject.

Looking from one to the other, Harry was struck by the utter normalcy of their lives. Whatever financial problems they might be experiencing, whatever schedule they had worked out for bringing a child into the world, they were of little significance when weighed against the air of domestic tranquillity that obtained in this household. For a moment Harry wondered at why such a normal life was a goal that had eluded him. On the other hand, being a good cop, even being a bad one, and maintaining a successful marriage were not always compatible objectives. One had a tendency to cancel out the other. Harry only hoped that Owens and his wife would be able to make it in the future as they seemed to be doing now. Once again, he regretted that Owens had become his partner just because as far as he could see he was not the greatest asset to the institution of marriage—for himself or anyone else.

Before they left the house, Owens announced that he was first going to get into his costume.

"Wait until you see him," Mary Beth said, delighted that her husband would finally be able to demonstrate to Harry a talent that he had not yet witnessed.

Twenty minutes later Owens appeared, though if Harry had not known in advance it was the same man he would never have been able to identify him.

The man who stood before him no longer resembled a cop or indeed any member of respectable society. Here was a derelict who had undergone the ravages of a life lived entirely on the streets and in men's shelters. His clothes were naturally ragged, but they were also stained and exuded a powerful odor of alcohol and urine long since dried. The coveralls he wore were loose, precariously held up by a strand of rope, his flannel shirt was alternately patched, and riddled with gaping tears, and generally looked as though it had been worn so continuously that a razor would be required to remove it from Owens' body. But the *pièce de résistance* was the face, the way Owens had with makeup and a wig created a creature so pathetic, so lost, and so resigned to scorn and abuse that Harry was practically ready to stuff his grime-coated hands with all the money he had in his pockets.

Owens, Owens the cop at any rate, was maybe thirty-two, thirty-three years old; the man he had transformed himself into looked to be close to sixty, but a prematurely aged sixty. A beard straggled gray and limp from his chin, his eyes seemed rheumy, unfocused, his cheeks were ruddy as though from years and years of alcohol consumption, his lips were gray and chapped, his brow was gnarled. To complete the effect, he wore a hairpiece that sprawled wildly, tangled and dirty, on his scalp, sending loose strands over his ears where already graying tufts stuck out.

And his walk had altered; he shambled, a bit hunched over, dragging one leg slightly behind the other as though he'd never quite recovered from an old wound in that limb. Saying nothing, he extracted a pack of cigarettes from his shirt pocket, dug out the last remaining cigarette, which was bent in the middle, and parked it between his lips. No sooner had he managed to light it than he started a dreadful hacking cough that persisted long enough to nearly double him up.

Harry watched all this with astonishment. The cough itself was incredible. He nearly believed that the real-life Owens was suffering from some terrible bronchial disorder, TB maybe. But no, suddenly Owens stopped his coughing, smiling broadly under his unruly mustache. "Well, what do you think?"

Harry shook his head in wonder. "I'm impressed."

Mary Beth stood alongside Owens, proud at how well he had mastered the art of deception.

"You should see me when I play the Creature from the Black Lagoon."

"This will do fine. Jesus, you make a better bum than the bums do themselves."

"Comes with practice," Owens laughed, consulting his watch, a Seiko well hidden under his shirtsleeve, then checking his .38 which was tucked safely out of sight beneath the waistband of his coveralls. "Everything where it should be," he declared.

Mary Beth kissed him—on the cheek so that she would not ruin the lipstick he'd employed to make his lips look so pallid. "You take good care of him, you hear," she told Harry.

"I certainly will do my best."

"And any time you feel like a home cooked meal, you know where to come."

"You don't know what you're saying," Harry told her, "you'll never see the end of me."

Chapter Four

In the past five and a half months the Mission Street Knifer had struck at several locations in the vicinity of the Greyhound Bus Station, on Market and Seventh, on Sixth and Mission, on Fourth, proximate to the Santa Fe and Western Pacific Depot, on the corner of Fulton, and farther south on Howard. The last time he had attacked was the fourth of October at quarter past two in the morning. His victim had been an elderly black of indeterminate age; he could have been anywhere from sixty to eighty-five. He was evidently sleeping on a bench inside the Greyhound terminal itself. The Knifer ended his life quickly enough, gouging out his throat immediately below the Adam's apple, but in keeping with his notorious reputation, he had not stopped there but had proceeded to slash open the man's chest possibly with the intention of tearing out the heart—a favorite habit of his—but had failed to do this, perhaps because he feared interruption. The results had been messy enough regardless, and the supervisory staff of the terminal was thankful that if this sort of mayhem had had to occur it was done at an hour when no one else was around to suffer the spectacle or, worse, the knife thrusts of the psychopath who regularly stalked those who were most helpless and beaten down.

The Mission Street Knifer was talented, if that's the word for it. He left no clues behind. Moreover, the victims he chose, even if they survived his deadly assaults, were often drunks, people whose minds were so generally befuddled or riddled with holes that they made for the most unreliable witnesses conceivable.

With nothing to go on, lacking first-person reports of what their knifer might possibly look like, Harry had no special strategy to implement in apprehending him. He asked Owens if he'd done something like this before.

"Well, not with a murderer, no, but I've worked as a decoy on cases involving muggers, pickpockets, prostitutes, that sort of thing."

"So you've worked in this area before?"

"Oh yeah, sure. I could give guided tours, though who'd want to take a guided tour in this district I don't know."

Harry gave him a pocket radio. "There may be times we'll be out of eye contact. Anybody gives you any trouble, even if you just sense some son of a bitch is going to give you trouble, signal me. We don't know what we're looking for. I suspect we'll catch a lot of fish and have to throw most of them back in before we find our man."

Though Owens took what he said at face value—that it was the Mission Street Knifer he was referring to—Harry actually meant not him so much as the murderer from the Tocador Hotel. Still, ridding the streets of the Mission Street Knifer would not be the least accomplishment of his career.

To complement the butt-end of a cigarette that dangled from his lips, Owens added a pint bottle of Wild Turkey. "It helps to look as vulnerable as you can," he said. He swallowed a bit of it so that his mouth would smell of the alcohol, spilled out another half to make it seem as if he'd been drinking for a while, then slipped it back into his jacket pocket. His jacket was as torn and frayed and stained as what he wore underneath it.

Harry drove him to a spot on the corner of Geary and Market. Then unfolding a map of the city he indicated the area that he wanted covered, which comprised approximately four square blocks.

"Don't wander farther afield, I want to be able to get to you fast if necessary."

Owens nodded, then when no one was nearby, quickly got out of the car and began his shuffling walk in the direction of Third.

Harry watched him until he was out of sight. Then he, too, emerged from his car, lackadaisically proceeding the same way. He wanted Owens to get the feel of the place without being distracted. His was a role for an audience other than his partner.

While the Mission Street Knifer generally kept late hours, timing his attacks for when there were few people on the streets save the derelicts who had no home to go to, it was not unknown for him to perform his gruesome business earlier in the evening, just so long as it was dark, just so long as his victims were alone.

Owens had the actor's knack of becoming what he was playing. One part of him, of course, remained the undercover police officer, cautious, constantly scrutinizing those he passed in the streets, ever prepared to react to danger if it should present itself, but the other part was a bum, drunk and stumbling, looking for a handout. No question that Owens had mastered his role. From time to time he muttered under his breath, cursing mindlessly, jettisoning great gobs of phlegm from his mouth.

There were others doing the same thing, but they were doing it for real. They were so lost in their own beleaguered worlds that they scarcely gave him a glance. He obviously had no money to give them. Once or twice, however, one would come up to him and entreat him for some of his bourbon.

Owens willingly would have given them some—his heart went out to these people whose bleak lives he was attempting to duplicate for a few hours—but that might mean becoming trapped in a conversation. These derelicts were often as hungry for talk, for any sort of companionship, as they were for booze or money. So he refused them all, acting like a cantankerous, embittered man too far gone on alcohol to endure the society of his fellow man.

He had to keep himself isolated. The Mission Street Knifer would not risk taking on more than one at a time, at least that was what his M.O. had thus far revealed.

"Hey, daddy," someone called to him.

He grumbled, kept right on going.

The man who'd just addressed him was a strapping fellow, maybe nineteen or in his early twenties, too handsome and cocky for his own good, with black hair slicked down with an oily lotion that made it glimmer in the pale light from the streetlamp overhead. He was wearing a leather jacket and jeans.

Trouble, Owens concluded.

The man strode up to him. Roughly, he nudged Owens' shoulder with his hand, forcing him off the sidewalk.

"I was talking to you, daddy. Whaddya say?"

Owens glared at him, muttering, "Fuck outta way," and continued to walk.

The young man was not about to let him get away. His mouth was working hard as he chewed his gum. "You got a little scratch on you, whaddya say? You got a little scratch? I know all about you fuckers, you make like you're poor when you're rolling in it, right? Am I right or what? Suckers feel sorry for you, they lay all this bread on you." He pushed Owens harder this time, almost toppling him over. "I know what your game is, I know your little act."

While he correctly guessed that it was an act Owens was performing, he had entirely mistaken its nature. Now he positioned himself directly in front of Owens, blocking his way. Owens was by temperament a patient man, so he resisted the impulse to do anything rash. Besides, if he was going to have to make an arrest he wanted the charge to stick. Accosting a police decoy and pushing him off the curb was hardly likely to cause a judge to slap much of a fine on the man. He'd probably be let off with a reprimand. So Owens merely tried to circle around him.

This strategy did not work. The man, with surprising speed, roughly threw Owens to the ground, kicking him twice in the ribs. Still Owens didn't do anything. He was waiting until the man stole from him which would add robbery to the assault and battery charges he was already liable for. Despite the pain that the kicks had produced, Owens looked forward with pleasure to making this arrest.

Now the man, thinking that he had this derelict adequately subdued, bent down and began rummaging through Owens' jacket pocket, coming up with a few pennies and one dime. He regarded them disdainfully, and flung them to the ground. "Fuckhead, you got more, fuckhead. I know you do."

He had just started his search through another pocket, though because it was so shredded it wouldn't have held anything in the first place, when he felt the cold barrel of a .356 Magnum pressed up against his temple.

In a voice that was distinctly unlike the boozy wavering voice he'd used a minute ago, Owens said, "Game's over now. Hands over your head."

"Now wait a—" But the would-be robber was too stunned to complete the sentence. Grudgingly but quickly, he did as he was commanded. Owens lifted himself from the gutter, maintaining his gun on his assailant.

"You are under arrest."

"Arrest?"

Owens dug his badge out of an inside pocket. "Police officer," he added gratuitously.

"Aw shit," the man muttered, aghast that his luck should have turned out so badly tonight.

Owens, out of the corner of his eye, spotted Harry who now came rushing toward him from up the block.

"What've you got?" he asked.

"Assault and battery, malicious mischief, robbery," Owens replied matter-of-factly. "Not the Mission Street Knifer but what the hell?"

Harry handcuffed the man. "Read him his rights," he instructed Owens, weary of having to go through the routine again himself. "We'll lock him up in the car, let him stew in his own juices for a while. Otherwise, we'll be running a shuttle to the station all night long."

Once they had installed the misguided assailant in the back of their car, they returned to the streets. Harry, unlike Owens, did not act remotely pleased by their catch. He had the feeling that this sort of thing was going to keep on happening and that by the end of the night they'd have a vanload's equivalent of perps but no Mission Street Knifer. And the trend might continue for several weeks' running until they had every vandal, every nickel-and-dime mugger and pickpocket, cleaned up from the Mission and Market Street area. That might be a nice civic accomplishment, but it would annoy the hell out of the overworked night judges who'd keep having to book these clowns and deal with them. And it wouldn't for a moment stop the murders and mutilations the Knifer was responsible for. About the best it would do would be to keep the Knifer off the streets for a while or induce him to find an area of the city less favored by police decoys.

For Owens, however, a catch was a catch. Bruised ribs were worth the price of admission. There were times when Owens missed his old acting career. This activity gave him an opportunity to relive those days in Los Angeles when he had been obliged to recite idiotic lines from stupid scripts. Here, at least, all the lines were his.

Two uneventful hours passed with Owens wandering back

and forth along the same dark, mournful streets in an apparent alcoholic daze. Periodically, he would sight Harry but would proceed on his way, completely ignoring him. Now and then he would slump down on a bench or curbstone and pretend to guzzle his pint bottle of Wild Turkey.

Buses continued to pull out and into the Greyhound depot with monotonous frequency, filling the air with exhaust fumes. People who'd just debarked wandered out onto Market, overburdened with luggage, trying to shake off the trance you get from hours and hours of traveling America's expressways.

Then, as though on cue, the activity subsided; fewer buses came and went, and there were many less people to be sighted on the streets in the depot's vicinity. The October night had become chillier, clouds scudded across a nearly full moon which soon dipped below the horizon, eliminating one very important source of light.

Way in the distance, Owens detected the sound of voices, boisterous and assertive. Three figures came into view, swaggering, for at this gray desolate hour they knew they had control over the streets, and they were determined to assert that control to anyone with whom they came into contact.

In keeping with the plan of operation, Owens was alone, a solitary bum who stood revealed in the harsh glare of a parking lot's solar lights.

Three black youths this time, jobless probably, bored no question, looking for a thrill to pass the time. Owens realized that he was about to become that thrill.

This time he was more apprehensive; it was not one-on-one as it had been before. He could not allow these three to gain too much of an advantage or he might be deprived of a chance to get at his gun.

Of course, it was always possible that they'd simply abuse him verbally and pass him by. But Owens had an instinct for these things, and he didn't believe there was much likelihood of that.

"Hey, baby, what've we got here?" the middle one asked.

"Looks to me like we got one unhappy sucker," another replied.

"Hey, sport, how you doin'? You gonna do a little jig for us?" the third addressed Owens.

"Sport, sport, I'm talkin' to you!" he said when Owens failed to respond. "You gonna give us a drink of your Wild Turkey?"

They were close to him now, forming a semicircle around him, their eyes mocking, their mouths curled into wide gleaming smiles.

The tallest of the three—he was maybe six-five—reached out to take hold of the bottle Owens held hugged to his chest. Owens, mumbling to himself, turned away, rebuffing him.

"Sport," he said, "that's not being polite. We all gotta share in this life. Ain't that right?"

"That's right, bro," his companions agreed.

The tallest took a step forward, grabbing hold of Owens' arm in an attempt to force the bottle from his hand. Owens decided to let him have it. But this was obviously not going to satisfy the trio. After taking a long swig of the Wild Turkey, the youth did not then offer it to his companions but rather tipped it upside down so that it splattered on Owens, getting in his hair and dribbling down his face. Owens nearly retched at the overpowering smell of the booze and had to rub his eyes, into which it had leaked. Even so they stung furiously.

"Hey, sport, what's wrong with you? You sure do look a sight."

This was sufficient provocation for even the ordinarily patient officer. He staggered as far from them as he could get, which wasn't very far since they continued to hound him in an ever diminishing circle.

Then he struggled to get his gun free.

"Hey, sport, what are you doin', you lookin' for your pecker?"

The laugh was derisive and far too loud.

One of his friends, obviously the moderate among them, looked a bit disgusted with the proceedings. "Hey, Sam, that's enough, fuck him, let's get out of here."

The man he'd called Sam, however, obviously had no intention of abandoning his prey. "You quittin' on me, Amos?"

Owens, while this exchange was taking place, managed to lay his hand on his Magnum, but he had yet to expose it to view, thinking that Amos might prevail on Sam to abandon his attack. If so, he'd let them go. He gave the third member of the party a searching look, trying to determine where he stood. Couldn't tell though; he was probably undecided, waiting to see the outcome of this dispute.

"I ain't quittin' on you, I just don't think we got to waste more time with this dude, that's all."

Suddenly Sam draped his right arm over Owens' shoulder, proclaiming with evident mockery, "This here is my good friend, ain't you my friend now?"

He shoved his face directly into Owens', his eyes gleaming with strange fascination. The question wasn't whether he was on drugs, the question was which drugs he was on.

"Hey, sport, what's wrong with you, you dumb piece of shit, you ain't answering my question."

Owens pulled away from him. Sam didn't like that. He pulled out a switchblade. The click as the knife flashed into the open was decisive. "You wanna find your pecker I'll find your pecker for you. I'll hand it to you on a platter."

"Ah shit, man," Amos said, deciding that this was nothing he wanted any part of. "You are a dumb motherfucker." He began walking away.

Sam was far too exhilarated by the thought of what he was about to do to Owens to do more than upbraid Amos for his desertion. He made no effort at retrieving him. The other youth that was left seemed to have made his decision: he was just going to stay where he was and watch. He looked like he anticipated a good show.

Because Sam expected no real resistance he was surprised, and a bit displeased, when Owens shrugged off his restraining arm. And when he lunged with his knife he wasn't too happy to find that this derelict was far more agile than a drunken derelict past his prime had any right to be.

But this disappointment was nothing compared to what he felt when Owens produced his gun and leveled it on him. "This is it, motherfucker!" Owens declared, using the epithet only because it seemed entirely appropriate to the circumstances and the vocabulary that Sam had thus far exhibited.

"Hey, sport, this is something else." Sam, unlike the youth on the sidelines, didn't appear to be intimidated by the sight of the gun. Otherwise he might have joined his friend and tried to run away. But even left to his own devices, Sam evidently lacked any fear. He also lacked any sense of reason, but that was something else entirely.

"Throw that knife down," Owens commanded with what he thought was an authoritative voice. "I'm a police officer. Throw that knife down."

"You is a po-leese officer?" Sam mocked. "Why sure you is."

He began to make circles in the air with his knife, neither advancing nor retreating. He was seeing whether he could out-psyche Owens.

"Am I going to have to shoot you?" Owens asked, tiring of this lunatic's games.

"Shoot me! Shoot me! Oh Jesus, yes, you are." Sam laughed again. His mind had been so monopolized by whatever shit he had driven into his veins or thrust up his nose that he may actually have wanted to find the wind whistling through a hole in his body come morning.

All at once he lunged forward, the switchblade just grazing the coveralls that drooped from Owens' shoulders. Owens didn't hesitate to fire.

The round from the .356 caught Sam in the thigh, severing an artery, or so Owens assumed from the sight of so much blood that erupted from the wound. Sam reeled back, but only because of the bullet's impact, not from any pain. Nor was he in shock. He was so far gone that his mind simply failed to register the pain.

Still, he was sufficiently in touch with reality to abandon any notion of coming at Owens again. He leaned against a parking sign, which didn't provide him with much support, and calmly, even indifferently, examined his wound. Blood continued to spurt out of it at such a terrific rate that Owens realized he'd bleed to death if he didn't receive medical attention soon.

Sam seemed somehow to understand what his predicament was now, for he finally relinquished his knife and gazed up at Owens with a sullen, contemptuous expression. "Motherfucker, you got my number, didn't you?"

When Harry finally arrived, having been alerted by the sound of the gunshot, he discovered Owens hard at work tying a tourniquet—improvised from his own stained coat—about the wound. "Son of a bitch dies, who knows what will happen," he was muttering. "We'll be accused of police brutality, cause a riot, blow this whole investigation to hell."

Harry realized he was absolutely right. He didn't have to ask what had happened. The sight of the switchblade on the ground was mute testimony to the reason Owens had fired.

He rushed back and got his car and brought it careening up to the curb where Sam lay sprawled, dazedly abusing Owens while his arterial blood, despite the constraint of the tourniquet, kept pumping out of him, dyeing his whole pants leg and much of the sidewalk a dark crimson.

They managed to get the injured man into the back of the car while their other prisoner looked on with bewilderment and consternation. "You fucking cops are too much," he declared, but whether he meant this as an insult or a compliment neither Harry or Owens could say.

For hours they waited, consuming Styrofoam cups of coffee to keep themselves awake. The dull green corridors leading from the Emergency Room were empty and silent save for the infrequent intrusion of a woman's mechanical voice paging one doctor or another. The nurses who were on this graveyard shift unfortunately weren't much to look at. They might have been efficient, but they all had the look of spinsters, their faces taut, their jaws defiant as they traipsed the corridors, bearing trays filled with sterilized instruments to be used in surgery. The odor that clung to the walls was appropriately antiseptic; the floors gave off a strong whiff of ammonia.

Technically, Harry and Owens had concluded their work for the night. It was five in the morning, a little past actually, and now that they had consigned one suspect into the hands of the law and the other into the hands of the surgeons, there was no reason they couldn't simply go home.

Except that Owens refused to leave, because he didn't want Sam Aikens (for that, his wallet indicated, was his last name) dying on him. Not that he was a sentimentalist; he just feared the repercussions. And somehow Harry couldn't bring himself to leave Owens by himself. Moreover, he shared Owens' concern. Any incident that might trigger a racial disturbance, anything that could provoke Bressler to take them off the case, was to be taken very seriously.

"This is lame, I realize it," Owens said. "I mean, here it is five o'clock in the goddamn morning, and we're sitting here praying that this bastard makes it when it's obvious that the world would be better off if he didn't. And what good are we doing here? Our presence isn't helping him any."

He looked down to the end of the corridor where the Emergency Room was situated. No telling what was going on in there. They could see only a hazy light through a small oval window.

"You want to leave, Drake?"

"No."

"Didn't think so."

"How long you think this is going to take?"

"Depends. They run into trouble, get a lot of bleeders, there's no way to know."

But at precisely that moment a surgeon, draped in green, his mask hanging down on his chest, appeared at the door to the Emergency Room. He gestured to the two officers. From his expression it was impossible to discern the outcome of the operation.

When they had approached close enough for him to speak, he said, "Well, he's going to be limping for some time to come, but he'll pull through."

Owens turned to Harry, his face lighting up like a child at Christmastime. "You hear that? You hear that? The fucker is going to make it!"

He was so exhilarated that he threw his arms first about the surgeon, then about Harry. "The goddamn son of a bitch is going to live!" he said. The surgeon meanwhile watched him in confusion, unable to comprehend why Owens was simultaneously cursing his patient and exhibiting unrestrained joy at the news that he would recover. It was clear from the way he looked at the two, and one of them in torn clothes that smelled powerfully of Wild Turkey, that he regarded cops with great skepticism. "Next time you want to stop somebody," he said to them both, "try the kneecap. You want to kill him, well, that's a different story."

"No, you got it wrong, Doctor," Harry said. "It's the same story, always the same story."

The surgeon shrugged. "I'll take your word for it. I don't have to take care of dead people."

Chapter Five

When it got to be quarter past eight and he still hadn't shown, Martha Denby began to get worried. He was usually so prompt. But she needn't have become alarmed. There was a loud rapping on the door to her suite.

She rushed to it, threw it open, threw her arms around her guest. "Teddy!" she said, "I thought you'd never come."

He clasped her to him, then relinquished his hold so that he could shut the door. "I must apologize. I am afraid I was held up. But to expiate, let me present you with this." From behind his back he produced a bottle of Piper Heidseick champagne. "I thought we might indulge ourselves."

"I think indulgence is the order of the evening," Martha said, hurrying into the small kitchenette to find an opener and a couple of long-stemmed glasses.

Though Martha was casually attired, having no plans to leave her room this night, she was still very conscious of the impression she made. She wore a black-striped T-shirt with slightly baggy tuxedo-striped pants, designed in Paris by Claude Montana.

Teddy always preferred that his women dress elegantly for him, and he went to great lengths to ensure that they did, never balking when they asked him for money to go shopping, no matter how exorbitantly priced the clothes and accessories they wanted were. And Martha also had remembered to sprinkle herself with Opium, a fragrance that she knew Teddy liked.

"How was the shooting today?"

She sighed. "Can't we talk about another subject?"

"You know I'm interested, Martha." He seated himself on the edge of the bed and began to work the cork out from the bottle. Before she could answer, the cork leaped up to the ceiling with a great pop, and a small geyser of champagne bubbled to the surface, dousing Teddy's hands.

Martha, laughing, took his hands and licked them clean.

But while this gesture certainly pleased Teddy, he insisted on returning to the subject of the film she was starring in.

"Yesterday was perfect. Today we were back to square one. That scene I do with Jim? Gus isn't pleased with it. Why do I have to get every goddamn perfectionist director in the business?"

"You learn that way," Teddy said, trying to soothe her. "You have to develop your career, gain experience. I keep telling you that."

He slapped her rump good-naturedly as though to punctuate his remark.

She looked momentarily sullen. "I don't know," she said.

"Is my favorite girl going to give me a smile?" Teddy poked her lips with a finger. And just as he requested, a smile formed almost against Martha's will. Right now she did not especially feel very fun-loving. But with Teddy, there really was no choice. Fun was all he wanted.

"Come sit beside me," he urged.

She complied, taking from him a newly filled glass of champagne.

"Now what shall we drink to?" he asked.

"To a speedy wrap of the film."

The glasses clinked.

"I tell you what, Martha. As soon as the shooting's completed, you and I will go to Acapulco for a couple of weeks, what do you say to that?"

"Just the two of us?" She was startled. Teddy rarely could afford to spend more than a couple of hours with her; that he should suggest a couple of weeks was little short of astonishing.

"What about your work?"

He shrugged. "Wouldn't you say I deserved a vacation?"

She kissed him sweetly on the lips. "No one deserves it more."

"But there is one other consideration."

"Oh?" She looked at him sharply. "And what's that?"

"It has nothing to do with me. It's Jim."

"Jim," she said with a certain bewilderment as if she'd completely forgotten about him. Then, suddenly quite serious, she turned to Teddy. "It's like this, Teddy. I like Jim. He's a dear boy, but what we have together is nothing like what I have with you."

"Just a typical Hollywood affair that'll end when the shoot is done?"

"Teddy!" she reproached him, irritated by the sarcasm that tinged his voice. "You know very well that I do not engage in 'typical Hollywood affairs.' "

Teddy did not immediately respond. "Am I to conclude then that Jim will pose no obstacle to your accompanying me to Mexico?"

"I do what I want. Jim does not control my every move or otherwise you wouldn't be here."

Teddy nodded with satisfaction. He had to be continually reassured that he had no rivals, no competitors, or that those he did have were mere playthings, likely to be discarded when the woman in question tired of them. But he made it amply clear that for his part if there were any discarding to do, it would be on his initiative not hers. Only occasionally did women fail to live up to his expectations: a severe miscalculation.

Abruptly, Teddy rose from the bed and walked to the window. They were high enough up, because of the hotel's height and because it was built on Nob Hill, for the view to be suitably panoramic. The bright lights from the North Beach area glimmered in the distance like a galaxy countless millions of miles away.

Martha joined him shortly and wrapping her left arm about his waist and snuggling close to him asked him what he was thinking. Asking Teddy what he was thinking was like asking the same question of a giant black bear that suddenly looms in your path. You would neither hope for an answer nor persist in the inquiry.

So Martha resigned herself to Teddy's shift in mood. Was he still angry about Jim? She'd thought they had gotten that out of the way. But with Teddy it was impossible to tell what was bothering him. She knew so little about his life to begin with.

"If I ever suspect that you stay with me because of your career," he said at last, "I will never forgive you."

She pressed herself against him. "No, no, it's not that at all. You know me better than that." She sought his lips with hers, desperate to get him to relax.

The truth was, of course, that her career had been one of the more compelling reasons why she had responded to his overtures. But things had changed since then. She found that she did love Teddy. Not love exactly. It was something greater and lesser than love, something that she had not experienced before, a kind of pressing need, an addiction. With Teddy she had a sense that she had embarked on an unusual adventure, one that would take her into forbidden realms that men like Jim Corona could never imagine, let alone assert mastery of. But to convince Teddy of this was infuriatingly difficult. When she'd been secretive and failed to tell him about the other men in her life he'd somehow found out about them anyway. But now that she was completely open with him, he seemed no less suspicious. There was no winning either way.

He was softening, his body, if not his mind, responding to her seductive posture. That was about as much as she could hope for. There was a rigid core that she would never break through, and though there were times that she tried she realized that if any woman would ever succeed at it it would not be her.

His hands gripped her ass, and with the power they had they practically lifted her whole body up against him. When he began to explore the supple contours of her back, her skin erupted as much in reaction to the coldness of his palms as to the excitement of the touch itself.

When, twenty minutes later, he had adjusted his trousers and tucked his shirt firmly in so that his appearance would in no way betray how he'd just spent his time, he gently reached down to where the blankets and sheets had collected in a heap and somehow succeeded in unravelling the tangled mess. Then he raised the reddest of the two red blankets and hoisted it along the length of Martha's unclothed body, drawing it finally over her head. He stepped away as if to better inspect what he'd accomplished.

Just then Martha, giggling, mumbled something under the covers.

Teddy good-humoredly uncovered her head. "What did you say?"

"I said I couldn't breathe," she was still laughing.

"Air as a means of sustenance is highly overrated," he said, butting his head down suddenly so that it was squashing both her breasts. With his lips he cradled the nipple of her left breast, allowing his teeth to tease the hardened protrusion as though he intended at any moment to bite it off. Then he withdrew, an unshakable calmness reflecting itself on his face.

In the dimness, and in such proximity, it was difficult for

Martha to discern much more of his face than the luminous intensity of his eyes bearing down on her.

Then he stood up, put on his jacket. "So I shall see you tomorrow at the same time?" he said, never thinking that she could possibly raise an objection. "I promise to be prompt."

"I don't think so, Teddy. Tomorrow's Halloween. The cast is throwing a party, and there'll be the parade. You could come if you want."

"Halloween, yes, I'd forgotten," Teddy said, a bit disgruntled that a mindless celebration should get in the way of his evening tryst. "Enjoy yourself then. We will do it Friday."

"Friday, yes, that'd be terrific." Though she didn't want him around she still felt obligated to ask him again if he'd like to attend the party with her.

"You know what I think about parties. My presence would only weigh on you, you wouldn't enjoy yourself."

"Oh, Teddy, don't say that. You know it's not true."

He let himself out. "Good-night, Martha. See you on Friday."

Chapter Six

Halloween. Though darkness hadn't settled in on the city, witches and ghosts were already on the march down Polk Street, making their way to parties or preparing to join the parade that would advance through downtown.

This was a night that the San Francisco police force generally dreaded. When people disguised themselves they felt protected in their anonymity, and they often acted in ways they would never think of when wearing their own clothes. The spirit of the night, with its vaguely sinister and pagan connotations, only heightened the possibility that someone might go off the deep end. And, in any case, there was always more danger whenever large numbers of people got together.

So the police were determined to make their presence well known and prior to the start of the parade the blue-and-white patrol cars, with "Police Services" imprinted on their chassis, and the less conspicuous black-and-white ones could be sighted everywhere along the parade route and on important intersecting streets.

It was Harry who suggested that tonight when they searched for the Mission Street Knifer they might consider straying farther from the drabber precincts surrounding the Greyhound Bus Station.

"Why would we want to do that?" Owens asked.

"I wouldn't be surprised if our Knifer takes advantage of the parade, maybe dresses in a costume himself. Could be that one reason he keeps to the Mission and Market Street area is that he knows anywhere else he'd stick out. But tonight nobody, no matter how bizarre-looking he is, is going to stick out. Not with the crowd we'll be getting."

"Oh? I missed last year's festivities. Is it really that crazy?"

"Let's just say it won't be easy to forget."

Owens was agreeable to the change in geography. He wasn't especially partial to the neighborhood he'd had to roam last night. And since they had no real leads to go on what did they have to lose?

He found it ironic, and rather comical, that for once his own personal costume party was being duplicated by tens of thousands throughout the city. Halloween was an occasion when everybody could play decoy if they so chose.

Harry, however, as always went as himself: the weary and skeptical Inspector #71.

Each year the parade seemed to get longer, and tonight it was strung out for blocks. Ghosts, witches, warlocks, skeletons, Space Age creatures bedecked in silver foil, characters out of *Star Wars,* women festooned in silver and white, a larger-than-life Marie Antoinette, her giant head bobbing, a sixty-piece brass band, men in Richard Nixon masks, one after another, they just kept coming, their passage announced by whistles, drums, and frequent renditions of "When the Saints Go Marching In."

Floats—of immense multisegmented snakes, of a gigantic skeleton whose torso and skinny white limbs moved in time to the music that sailed up into the air—were borne aloft by the crowd as it progressed down Van Ness. Thousands thronged into the street, cheering, expecting at any moment to be surprised and delighted anew by the continuing spectacle. In the distance, horns blared furiously as drivers trapped in the rerouted traffic protested their paralysis.

In his own car on Sacramento Harry listened to the familiar

female voice that dominated the police band. "Charlie 8, a 1080 on Pine. Woman says she's been robbed. That's the corner of Octavia and Pine. . . ." And from Charlie 8, the reply: "10-40," meaning that Charlie 8 would respond to the call rather than passing the responsibility along to another patrol car.

The calls kept coming in with increasing frequency: 1080s, 801s, 211s, thefts, suicides, robberies. . . . On a night like this, incidents of violence had a habit of breaking out with a certain momentum; it was as though there was some weird current in the air that prompted madness in one person and passed it on to another. It was more contagious than the bubonic plague and maybe just as virulent. A full moon Harry had found could do it, too.

Occasionally, Harry would check in with Owens. There was, after all, no way to keep visual track of him, not with the hordes that had descended into the city's center for the parade.

"Everything's fine here, Harry. Just a bit confusing," Owens would answer. In the background Harry could hear some of that confusion, a tumult of voices and jittery music.

"Where are you now, Drake?"

"Headed east on Golden Gate."

"10-4."

Harry decided to put his car in motion so that the distance separating him from his partner would not become too great. The problem was that with traffic blocked and detoured, it was difficult to get anywhere without protracted delays, and Harry was no luckier than most of the motorists who'd made the mistake of coming out on a night like this.

He got to Ellis half an hour later, and he was still three blocks from Golden Gate. He had not heard from Owens in the interim, and he thought he'd best raise him again on the radio and discover exactly where he was.

But he failed to receive a response.

"Drake, this is Alpha 2, do you read me?"

Nothing.

"Drake, this is Alpha 2, Harry Callahan here. Where are you?"

Nothing. Nothing but static and the intrusion of competing signals that somehow had jumped to his channel.

With passage impeded the way it was, Harry realized the futility of relying on his car any longer. While it was conceivable that the radio transmission was at fault, he did not believe it. Either Owens was in some danger or he was in a situation where he could not risk exposing his own radio to view. In either case Harry was sufficiently alarmed to park his car—which actually meant double-parking it—and proceed on foot.

In a half hour's time Owens could have wandered much farther afield. He might not be on Golden Gate at all any longer, but that was his last given location and so it was there that Harry determined he would first look.

Almost twenty blocks to the north and several blocks to the east, in a discotheque on the corner of Union and one of the streets intersecting it between Van Ness and Fillmore, a masked ball was well in progress. It was, to be sure, an unusual masked ball, appropriate to the 1980s in terms both of the costumes that the revelers had chosen and of the energy that they exhibited in carrying on their celebration. For instance, several individuals of both sexes displayed what might be called the "sick" or the "infirm" look; these people came gauzed and bandaged, in wheelchairs, or limping with the aid of walkers. One man arrived in a fully electric rolling hospital bed; wowing the public while propped up on pillows.

But this was nothing compared to some of the more ingenious revelers who'd doused themselves in genuine animal blood, sold by a place called McDermott Meats in Oakland: the sight of them was repulsive enough, but it paled beside the smell.

And, of course, there were the usual ghouls and goblins and

many, many women in leotards, tanktops, floor-length gowns, all with faces painted to make them look as though they had been recently exhumed from their final resting place, except that the eyes had been darkened and the lips brightened in order to present a contrast to the pasty whiteness of the skin that surrounded them.

An actress to begin with, Martha Denby was practically unrecognizable, with a black mask that gave her the look of an executioner and a loose black garment that hung to her feet, from which sandaled feet protruded. Whenever she moved into the light, and there wasn't much reliable light in this place, anyone with an observant eye would notice that the black gown she wore was so fragile and gossamer that it was virtually transparent and that she had nothing on underneath. Nothing whatsoever.

In fact, the only way you could determine that this was Martha without hearing her identifiably lilting voice was by Jim Corona's anxious presence. He, dressed as a pirate, eye patch and big gold looped earring in left ear, never let her get farther than the outer limit of his own shadow.

If she was open with Teddy about Jim, she was not open with Jim about Teddy. He was more likely to leave her if she told him she was seeing another man, whereas Teddy regarded Jim patronizingly, thinking of him as a harmless boy who entertained Martha only so long as they were making a movie together. Teddy, Martha understood, felt that only he could successfully pleasure her. He naturally assumed that when the movie was over, and Acapulco loomed closer, that he had only to snap his fingers, and Martha would discard Jim without a second's hesitation.

Martha, when she was with Teddy, exulted in the excitement he aroused in her. But when she was with Jim she felt more comfortable, cozier. She could imagine settling down with him one day.

The specific problem she and Jim were encountering tonight was that she was hellbent on having a good time and Jim, despite his pirate outfit, seemed not to be in the spirit of the occasion. In fact, he was downright peevish and irritable. He wouldn't dance with her, and he made it clear that he resented her dancing with anybody else.

"You're a drag," Martha said and went off to dance anyhow, but for fear of agitating him further she made certain only to dance with flamboyant homosexuals who delighted in bedecking themselves in wild regalia: chains, keys hanging out, leather jackets, leather pants, leather boots, impenetrable dark glasses, motorcycle helmets, or sometimes just about nothing at all except some tiny trace of cloth that wound about their loins but left the cheeks of their buttocks fully revealed.

When she returned to Jim, she was drenched with sweat but happy and excited, and she wanted him to be excited, too. She wrapped her arms around him and drew him close to her. "Hey, Captain Kidd, what's wrong?" She kissed him, brushing his face with the vinyl of her mask.

"Nothing."

Refusing to release him, she said, "That's not true. You've been acting weird all night. What is it, something to do with the film?" She knew it wasn't the film, but she wanted to get him talking.

"Not the film. Nothing to do with the film."

"Then what?"

He could be restrained no longer. "There's somebody else," he declared, spitting the words out.

"What do you mean someone else?" she asked, feigning astonishment, though she knew exactly what he meant.

"Just what I said. You're seeing another man."

She promptly denied the accusation. "What led you to think that?"

"I can tell, I know."

"Have you been following me around?"

"Then it's true."

"I didn't say it was true. It's not true. But I want to know-whether you've been spying on me." What she was thinking was: I've already got Teddy spying on me, I don't need another one.

"Do you think I would have to spy on you to figure out you've been having it off with someone else. People have eyes, you know. They talk."

"Talk? Who talks? Margo? Sandy? Peter?" She was naming possible suspects among the cast and crew who might, just might, have heard something and who were too untrustworthy to keep a secret long.

"You're only digging yourself in deeper, Martha. You're as much as admitting you are. You are screwing another man, who is he?"

"I am not going to engage in this conversation a moment more."

She was furious, furious that her evening was being ruined and that her juggling act with Teddy and Jim might be in jeopardy. She decided that she would terminate the argument before it grew too heated.

So she wheeled about and stormed off into the crowd. At first Jim stood and watched her, then he rushed after her.

"Come back."

He caught hold of her arm.

"I'm going home."

"Let me take you."

"No."

It was impossible to carry on a conversation like this, since both of them were constantly being buffeted by dancers who weren't very happy about tripping over them.

Unlike the man Jim Corona played in the movie, the real-life Jim Corona could not persuade Martha either to remain with him or to allow him to accompany her.

He did not believe that she intended to go home. In fact, that was her plan. She wanted to mull things over, figure out how she could allay Jim's suspicions while at the same time determine whether there was a leak on the part of someone on the set or whether Jim was just acting on a hunch because of his own insecurity.

At the entrance to the disco, a fur wrap draped over her flimsy dress giving her protection from the autumn chill, she extended her arm to flag down a taxi, thinking that because the parade had drifted farther south in the city, and with the streets surrounding Union being freer of traffic, she would not have too long to wait.

But when after ten minutes no cab appeared, she gave up and began walking, mixing with noisy, costumed celebrants who thronged the pavement, delighting in the anonymity her costume gave her.

Then she felt a hand on her arm. Jim! she thought angrily. He'd chased her all this way. "I'm not going with you!" she shouted.

But when she turned she saw that it wasn't Jim at all. It was Teddy. Uncostumed.

He looked mildly surprised, more amused, and he said, "Oh no? Is that your final word on the subject?"

She was heartened to see him. "Teddy! What are you doing here? How did you recognize me?"

She still had not removed her mask. Unless he had followed her out of the discotheque there was no way he could have known who it was.

But all she got from him was his customary smile that suggested he knew the world and the ways people had of dealing with it far better than she. "It must be magic," he said.

"Magic? Were you watching me all this time?" She did not wish to provoke him by using the word spying. Teddy was not Jim Corona.

"I am always watching you. I find you lovely, in costume or out, and so I see nothing wrong with watching you."

She drew her wrap tighter around her. "Well, I don't like it."

She was thinking: He must have been in the discotheque, disguised, observing me and Jim.

He ignored her last remark. Instead he took her arm and began to guide her up the street. She did not resist. "Where are you taking me?"

"First to my car."

"And then?"

"Then to a very special place."

Because of the mask he could not see the dubious expression that had taken hold of her face. "You're crazy, Teddy," she said affectionately.

"I am at that," he agreed quite seriously.

Chapter Seven

Harry could not find Owens, not on Golden Gate, not on McAllister or Fulton, which ran parallel to it, not on Buchanan, Laguna, Webster, Steiner, or Octavia, which ran perpendicular to it. Among the stragglers who had detached themselves from the parade or had simply never caught up with it in the first place Harry could see no one who vaguely resembled the boozing, shambling derelict that Owens had become. Ghosts and Merlins, Jack the Rippers and Count Draculas, Frankensteins and vampires there were aplenty, even a few genuine bums who dazedly stared at such unusual exhibitionism, probably wondering whether what they were seeing had any basis in reality or was merely a result of hallucinations brought on by alcohol and the d.t.'s.

Harry kept going, having no time to admire the ingenuity of the disguises that greeted his eyes, half-running, half-walking, impatient with those that unwittingly impeded his progress. Every now and then he took out his radio and again attempted to establish communication with his partner. No luck.

Thirty-five minutes had been exhausted in this manner, and yet Harry had no intention of giving up his search even if he was obliged to call out an entire search party to join him in the effort.

Where, he thought, stopping now to catch his breath, where would he go to find trouble if trouble was what he wanted? It did not take him long to find an answer.

Golden Gate Park. There, with the woods and the brush and the dark, a man could commit his crimes, be they minor or major, without fear of discovery.

When he'd first seen him, Owens hadn't given him a second thought. He was just another man in mufti though his size was formidable. Draped completely in a thick cotton robe all of black, with a skeletal mask blotting out his entire face, he must have measured almost seven feet, but his height alone wasn't the most distinguishing thing about him. He was massive, and this massiveness was not useless fat and sagging flesh but muscle, sinewy and probably made tougher by rigorous exercise. To be sure, he attracted attention even among a crowd that was partial to eccentric disguises. If his size and weight failed to gain people's notice, the scythe he carried in his hand certainly did. You could believe that this was Death incarnate, coming to reap his grim harvest this Halloween eve.

Wherever he walked people drew aside to let him pass. Quite reasonably, no one had any wish, no matter how intoxicated they may have been, to provoke him to a quarrel.

On spotting him, Owen's first thought was: Too obvious. This cannot be our man.

But nonetheless, he proceeded to tail him, staying well behind, which presented no problem as this figure of Death was all too conspicuous.

At a certain point, however, as the man proceeded at a slow but steady rate it became apparent to Owens that he was headed straight into the park. Golden Gate was just about empty of pedestrians and traffic at this time of night. Although Death never looked back—and Owens never expected him to—it was no longer so easy to shadow him. After awhile they were the only two walking in the same direction.

Owens thought of how ridiculous it must look to an outsider; he imagined a painting entitled "Bum Chases Grim Reaper Who Won't Have Him."

Nonetheless, he was still wary and a bit frightened. It might look ridiculous, but he was beginning to think that his instinct had been on target, that whether this was the Mission Street Knifer or not, he was up to some mischief. So that he would run no risk of alerting Death to *his* true identity Owens turned his radio off. It might be simple paranoia on his part. He didn't know, but he hoped that Harry would understand his apprehension.

As they approached the park—with Owens half a block behind his mark—the lights grew fewer. Death at times seemed to be swallowed up in the gloom, but just when Owens figured he'd lost him he reappeared. He was making more noise now as brambles and fallen leaves crumpled noisily under his feet.

Owens was as quiet as he could be traversing the same terrain, but there was no way of avoiding making some noise. Still, the distance that separated them was such that Death did not notice, or noticing, care to investigate its origin.

Owens lost track of how much time he had invested in this enterprise. All he knew was that he was being led on a tour of the park that took him, improbably, into the Japanese Tea Garden. The two passed over a hand-carved gateway into the garden proper. Below them Owens could make out the reflecting pools, which were dark. Occasionally, their placid water would be disturbed by a fish coming to the surface, but otherwise these smooth bodies of water were like perfect mirrors, waiting for Death, whose form, hideous and immense, extended across the entire length of one pool.

Owens looked and saw that his image, too, was visible upon the water of the same pool. For an instant the two reflections collided and merged, but only for an instant. Then Death vanished, from the pool, from the other side of the graceful humpback bridge. All that Owens could make out on the other side were the dwarf trees and the moss-covered rocks but not Death. He could not see how he could have vanished like that, and so continued across the bridge himself, wondering whether he'd been spotted in spite of his precautions, wondering, too, whether Death wasn't waiting in ambush for him, ready to put his intimidating instrument to use.

But Owens plodded on, too committed to this venture to allow his fears to deter him. Nowhere was his man Death visible on the bamboo-railed paths, but he felt certain he must be close by. As he kept going, various statues intended to guard the Shinto shrines came into view. And for a moment Owens felt that their sightless eyes were in fact registering his presence just as they had registered Death's. Farther on, he came to a seated bronze Buddha whose serene countenance intimated at an existence far more secure than that of the average San Francisco cop.

As Owens came nearer the Buddha, Death suddenly, silently materialized and just as silently strolled away. Only the rustle of the manicured bushes that he brushed past told Owens that he was not just a hallucination. The way he seemed to glide, this dark menacing figure, was almost as if he was otherworldly, without substance, though of course he was very much substance, all seven feet and two hundred eighty pounds (Owens guessed) of him.

So he followed him, despairing that he would ever be rewarded for his efforts. Followed him throughout the park, to Stow Lake favored by picknickers and boaters, past the Conservatory, down along Arguello Boulevard, past the Arboretum on South Drive, now onto the archery field. . . .

This is getting absurd, Owens realized, he's just going to keep walking all night, and Harry will think I'm an ass for playing along with him. But it was also possible that Death was acutely conscious someone was stalking him—in tiring, Owens recognized that he might have unwittingly betrayed himself—and was only seeing how far he could take him.

From the archery field Death made his way to the golf course that lay adjacent to it. Because the green was so exposed Owens was obliged to stick close to the woods and shrubbery that extended about a good part of its perimeter. At a certain point though he had no choice but to give up his place of concealment. Otherwise, he would lose sight of Death again.

The odyssey was growing endless. Death had sufficient stamina to endure what constituted a grand tour of Golden Gate. Owens no longer had much of a sense of where they were anymore. He could not orient himself by any landmark. Here was a baseball field, here a football field, here a tennis court, over there a checker pavilion. Now the smell of horse manure told him he was nearing a stable; now he found himself in the shadow of a bandstand that at this late hour looked particularly desolate. There are twenty-seven miles of footpaths in Golden Gate Park, and by one in the morning Owens had the feeling that he and Death had traversed them all.

Then, in a thickly wooded area that bordered on a baseball diamond, Owens looked up to see that Death had vanished again. Was he not paying enough attention? How could he have slipped so easily out of view? Owens peered into the gloom, thinking that maybe in his dark robe Death had managed to camouflage himself.

Owens started towards the woods, deciding that he would draw out his gun. He was more nervous now than he had been any time since he had begun this surveillance, though he could not say why. After all, Death had dematerialized before, in the Japanese garden, and nothing had happened.

Owens stopped, listening, straining his eyes to detect a pattern in the darkness, but everything was submerged and ambiguous in the absence of any light. Even the moon was uncooperative, having sunk out of sight hours ago.

Cicadas he heard, the disturbance of lowlying brush as some animal, possibly a squirrel, darted through it, that he heard. But otherwise nothing.

Until a moment later, when the unmistakable sound of footsteps, soft but firm and purposeful, reached his ears from behind him. He turned, quickly, no longer bothering to maintain the pretense of a drunken derelict lost in the park, his gun trained on the direction from which the footsteps were coming.

It was Death all right, looming up in front of him, seeming taller, more formidable than he had ever appeared in the distance. How he had gotten in back of Owens Owens couldn't possibly imagine, but that was hardly worth worrying about now.

The sight of a .356 Magnum did not seem to intimidate Death. It was difficult to tell whether he even noticed it. And while Owens struggled to announce that he was a police officer, he wondered on just what charges he could engineer an arrest. Despite his terrifying aspect and his penchant for straying for hours through the precincts of Golden Gate Park armed with a scythe, Death had not committed anything that could remotely be considered a crime.

Nonetheless, Owens had been a cop long enough to know that even without rational grounds for suspicion, this was a dangerous character who, with each step he took closer to Owens, seemed to get progressively more dangerous.

"Police officer, stay where you are." Owens wondered whether he'd made himself heard, his voice sounded so feeble. Compared to this, last night's confrontation with a surly white asshole and a drug-crazed black was child's play. He regretted that he'd gone so far in tracking this man down.

There was nothing to indicate that Death had heard him. The skeletal mask he wore made it impossible for Owens to determine if there'd been any reaction. He repeated himself, more loudly.

Still didn't make any difference. Death kept coming, inexorably closing the distance that separated them until they were no more than five or six feet apart. Owens realized that he ought to stand his ground, but he could not help backing away. Besides, if Death got right up on top of him he would have no room to maneuver or to fire his gun if he was forced to do so.

Death produced a sound that might have been laughter, but whatever it was it was obscured by the blockage of the mask. He now leaped forward, mocking Owens' efforts to retreat, and as he did this he raised his fearsome weapon above his head and swung it so that it described an arc, which if completed would take a substantial chunk out of Owens' neck.

Owens instinctively shifted his body to the left, discharging his gun at the same time. But because he did not shift quite enough, the blade grazed his shoulder. A savage burning pain caused him to cry out, but he retained his balance and ignored the blood that welled quickly from the wound.

There was no question, given his aim and their proximity, that he had hit Death. The blood that now appeared on the black robe, right where his pelvis should be, indicated to Owens that the bullet had penetrated. The sight of it also reassured Owens that his antagonist was human, something he was almost ready to doubt.

But while he might have been a mortal, Death surely did not act like one. The wound might not have been there at all, for he continued to advance on Owens, swinging his scythe back and forth, almost in a leisurely manner, without any aim of striking Owens. He seemed to be enjoying the swishing sound it made through the air as though he was trying to terrify Owens further before dealing him a decisive blow.

Owens, however, had no intention of waiting around for that. He maintained a steady pace backward so that the distance between the two of them never grew too small. "Stop right there or I'll fire again," he declared.

But Death kept coming. Owens did as he promised, firing into what he thought must be the man's stomach. Death grunted, but that was all. His momentum was not hampered the least bit. And again Owens fired and again.

At least Owens had the satisfaction of seeing that his bullets had hit their mark each time, for now there were four patches of blood on the folds of the black robe, two at chest level, one in the abdomen, the last in the thigh. Soon the blood stains began to merge until half the front of Death was covered. It looked as though someone had painted him with crimson paint just to contrast with the black background.

Owens was astonished, and not a little horrified, to see that though he'd been successful in hitting the man, he had failed to bring him down. Death again lunged, bringing down his instrument hard, but this time Owens was more agile and leaped out of its way altogether, firing once more, this time in the direction of the head. But because of his sudden movement the trajectory the bullet took brought it into the upper chest. Again Death emitted a sound that Owens construed to be a cry of pain, but that was all. The blood from this, the highest wound on his body, trickled slowly down his robe. But he kept right on coming.

There would be no time to insert another clip into his gun, Owens realized, and unless the cumulative effect from these five wounds soon took hold and Death collapsed, he might not escape after all.

Moreover, the injury he'd sustained was agonizing him, though it probably wasn't very serious. While Death might be able to endure so much pain and loss of blood, he doubted that he could.

He began to run, but still backward because he did not want to risk turning away from his assailant. But running backward in the dark is no easy thing to do. Suddenly, Owens stumbled over a branch that had broken off from a tree directly overhead. Though he struggled to regain his balance, it wasn't possible, and he fell awkwardly, sprawling in a plot of ivy. For a moment his gun loosened from his hand, but he was able to keep hold of it finally, not that it necessarily was going to do him very much good. For Death, more hideous than ever with blood dripping off him, was now looming over him, his scythe raised high before he brought it down on Owens.

Owens fired again, hitting him this time in the face, but while a part of the skeletal mask fell away, replaced by a big bloody hole, it was hardly the fatal wound Owens had hoped it would be. He realized that the bullet had probably penetrated the cheek, gone in one side and right out the other. When Death turned his head and Owens could glimpse the whole of it he saw that he was correct in his assessment: the bloody hole on one side of the mask was matched by a corresponding hole on the other.

This only caused this creature to appear more grotesque than before. What was he dealing with here, Superman? Owens wondered, rolling away from the scythe as it came down, slicing out a swath of ivy in the process.

But his reprieve was sure to be temporary. Death still commanded all the power in this situation. Could be he lacked all feeling, which was why none of the pain registered. Whatever explanation there was, it scarcely mattered to Owens who strained to get himself off the ground.

Death was slowing down somewhat, not much but enough so that when he swung again, the scythe failed to hit Owens and only struck the sole of his shoe as he scrambled to get up. A slice of the sole went flying into the air.

All at once Death, frustrated in his efforts to dispose of Owens, caught up with him and clasping him by the shoulders threw him back down to the ground. The pain that resulted from the gloved hand wrapped about his slashed shoulder more than the force his assailant applied was what disabled Owens.

Now it seemed it was all over, that he had come to the end, and that he now had no choice but to resign himself to his fate.

Chapter Eight

Harry, peering into the distance, beheld two figures, one a bloody spectacle clad in some kind of black garment, the other a blur of cloth and flesh supine on the ground. Of one thing he was certain—the man in the black robe was readying to kill his victim with a scythe.

It must be Owens, he reasoned. Hearing gunshots, he'd rushed as fast as he could in their direction. Now, without taking the trouble to aim carefully, there being no time, he fired his .44. He did not bring down the black-robed monster—for Harry recognized even from this distance that the size of this man was incredible—but he did distract him from his objective.

He fired again just as the black-robed figure turned to discover where this latest irritation was coming from. What astonished Harry was that this man did not do what anyone else would have done—bolted or ducked and taken cover. No, he just stood where he was, observing Harry's progress across the landscape with what might have been mild curiosity.

Then, abandoning Owens, he abruptly broke into a trot, evidently deciding that he would rather take on Harry instead. His speed was surprising. Behind him he left a zigzagging trail of blood on the grass.

For a moment Harry was too stunned to do anything. He

could not believe that anyone so bloodied could remain ambulatory. But the fact was that it looked worse than it actually was, for many of the bullets Owens had fired had failed to penetrate to vital organs, and instead had been absorbed by the fat and muscle that lay in the way.

With surprising speed, the scythe-wielding madman was upon Harry, flailing his weapon. Up close, he was a more grotesque sight than from across the field. The whole lower half of his mask was smeared with blood, which bubbled continuously from the slit that allowed his lips to show through.

Harry fired again from a crouch, calmly aiming at the man's chest. The blast did manage to slow the madman's momentum, sending him staggering back, his hands clutching at the latest wound. But much to Harry's astonishment it did not stop him. Redoubling his efforts, with a tenacity that was little short of miraculous, he came again at Harry and, just as Harry fired, whipped the scythe through the air, catching the gun with a sharp whack and with such force that it knocked the .44 out of Harry's hands.

Still, he had not been quick enough to forestall yet another wound, this time above the heart. He was lurching about like a drunk, barely capable of taking advantage of his triumph in relieving Harry of his weapon. Anger, sheer overwhelming anger, was all that was fueling him now. That and a determination to take somebody with him before he succumbed to all these wounds, which inevitably he would.

The .44 hadn't flown very far. Harry could glimpse it out of the corner of his eye: a gleaming object a yard or so over to his right. But there was no way he could retrieve it without risking his life.

So instead he assumed the stance of a quarterback and rammed right into the frenzied creature, something he obviously had not expected, for he tumbled over onto the ground, still gripping his scythe but finding it a clumsy thing to use effectively from such an awkward posture.

Nonetheless, Harry could feel its sting as the madman attempted to stab him with it. The point of it, however, never dug more than a fraction of an inch into Harry's skin since the man had not enough purchase to deliver any reasonably fatal blow.

Worse than the shots of pain that the tip of the scythe produced was the smell of blood that clung to every inch of the man. Harry was half-bathed in it, too, and he imagined that by now his antagonist probably had more blood outside him than in.

The madman clutched hold of him, as in an embrace, and it was difficult for Harry to extricate himself. Then, with a surge of energy, the madman somehow managed to roll over to his side, and Harry lost his advantage. With an arduous effort that betrayed his draining energy and blood, the madman raised himself to a vertical position. As he did he sustained two rounds in his back—both from Owens, who came racing in their direction, a new clip in his Smith and Wesson.

The first round caught Death in the hollow between the shoulder blades. The second lodged higher up in the neck, simultaneously severing the spinal cord and eliminating all sensation in his body—not that he seemed to have much to begin with.

These wounds appeared to have made some impact—the man could no longer move. His knees buckled and threatened to give way, but, maybe out of sheer obstinacy, he remained standing, swaying back and forth.

Harry, just now rising from his prone position, seized hold of Death's hand, tearing the scythe from his loosened fingers. Death hadn't the strength to resist any longer. Then Harry struck out with the scythe that his assailant would have preferred to impale him with, embedding it to halfway down the blade in the monster's chest, enough so that the tip of the instrument protruded out his back, which meant that a prodigious amount of flesh, muscle, fat, and inner organs had had to be gone through.

Death sagged, his legs finally did give way, but not before Owens, not more than six feet away, discharged his .356 straight into his head from the back. There was not enough tissue to protect the skull, and the rounds traveled through it without meeting much resistance, shattering the bone, opening up the brain, tearing it into bloody pulp-like shreds before emerging out through the face. All at once there was no longer anything to be seen of the mask, for an abundance of blood and gray matter and bone fragments came pouring out, obscuring what the bullets had not obliterated.

Death collapsed completely, falling on the scythe so that he pushed even more of the blade through his ravaged body. He didn't fall all the way, but rather remained partly suspended on it, just a few inches above the ground. Weirdly, he wasn't completely dead, though he was about as close as you could get without being there. Or maybe death just hadn't registered in some of the extremities because for a few moments a limb would twitch, a hand would reach tentatively out, then drop back again.

And then there was no more motion. Blood dripped noisily into the viscous pool that had already formed.

Death was at last truly dead.

For several seconds neither Harry nor Owens exchanged a word. What, after all, could they say?

Such was the awesomeness of this experience that both men had temporarily forgotten about their pain. Owens, who'd staunched the bleeding of one of his assailants the night before, now had to do the same for himself, tying a shred of coat over his shoulder which continued to bleed, though less profusely. The back of Harry's jacket had been ripped in several spots, and here and there blood could be seen in those places where the scythe had cut into the skin.

At last Owens spoke, "I don't know as to whether I've ever

seen anything like this. I didn't think the son of a bitch was going to die. One out of a million people could take what he did and still be walking."

"Try one out of a billion. This must have been what it was like bringing down Rasputin." Rasputin's assassins had variously tried to poison him, shoot him, drown him and leave him to die of exposure—all in the course of the same night. He just hadn't wanted to go out easily.

Now Harry reached forward and, ignoring the blood and disgorged tissue as best he could, drew away what was left of the mask. But that didn't do much good at all. There was so little remaining of the face that they would never know what he looked like.

"You think this is the Mission Street Knifer?" Owens asked.

"I don't know about that, but he's the leading contender for the role. Whatever he is, or was, the world's better off now that he's not around."

"Amen," said Owens with the reverence of a man who has witnessed a miracle. A perverse and horrible miracle but a miracle all the same.

Chapter Nine

The establishment that Teddy was taking Martha to was located on Folsom. Though it was open twenty-four hours a day and did not require any reservations, non-members were admitted only on Tuesday and Sunday evenings. This qualification made no difference to Teddy who was a dues-paying member and was, in any case, well known by the management from previous visits.

Friday nights had become known in this place as "hot and nasty nights," but even though it was still Thursday much of that hotness and nastiness was already present. Of course, the fact that it was Halloween occasioned a certain libertine spirit in excess of the usual.

And what went on here was practically anything. In front, there was a large public area where several people were immersed in a hot tub equipped like most hot tubs in town with a Jacuzzi. To the rear there were any number of saunas, but the hot tubs and saunas were not what one came here for.

The facilities were advertised as the most extensive in the city, though no doubt other entrepreneurs were busy running around trying to establish clubs more elaborate still. At any rate, an explorer, who was single-minded enough not to get distracted before completing his odyssey (and there was plenty to get distracted by), would also find a pinball room, with some of the latest video games installed, a snack bar, a porno-movie lounge, and for those with a longing for a good roast beef sandwich between excitements, even a delicatessen.

But again, all these features were just so much icing on the proverbial cake, for in addition to such public rooms there were thirty-six private rooms and three private "party" areas. And that was where the true business of the club went on. Whatever one's proclivity and taste, whether one was straight or gay or merely straddling the fence, one was almost certain to find someone suitable to provide satisfaction, at least for the duration of an hour, an hour being as long as you could rent a room.

As soon as Martha and Teddy entered the club, Martha understood at once just what kind of place it was. Because she had spent most of her time in the L.A. area, she had scant knowledge of San Francisco's nightspots, allowing Teddy and Jim and other members of the cast and crew to escort her around town. So she had no idea in advance of what she was getting into, and while she did not regard herself as the least bit prudish, she was not at all sure she wished to indulge herself in the public eye.

She was also, and quite justifiably, thinking of her reputation, though, as Teddy was quick to point out, there were so many people, so many bodies, that there was little likelihood that anyone would recognize her. Her flesh might surely interest them, but not her face.

"I thought we could just be alone," she said petulantly.

"Alone? Later we'll be alone. I have rented the Sun Room, and we can meet there in an hour or so and have all the solitude we want."

It was not this reassurance or the implication that she was free to do what she wanted in the intervening hour that silenced her but the recognition that it made no sense to argue with Teddy.

All she said was, "There's no sun. Why the Sun Room?"

"What's in a name?" Teddy said. "Remember, it's now eleven-thirty. Say by quarter to one meet me there."

"How will I find it?" She gazed around, and all she saw was flesh blurred by lots of steam.

"Ask anyone," Teddy said brusquely and then disappeared into the steam, anxious to try his luck with the anonymous free-spirited and impatient women who awaited the attentions of a man. Any man.

Martha, so abruptly deprived of Teddy's company, wasn't sure what she wanted to do. Still keeping her clothes on, she wandered from one room to the next, feeling strangely embarrassed by the exposure of flesh all about her and the unrestrained passions exhibited by couples of all sexes, clutching, moaning, fucking out in the corridors presumably because none of the thirty-six private rooms was available or maybe just because they felt like it. She stumbled into the porno-movie lounge. Marilyn Chambers was writhing frenetically on the screen, but from the strangled, fitful sounds that welled up from the audience Martha suspected that no one was paying too much attention to the film.

Pinball seemed like the safest bet, and Martha assumed that she could pass the remainder of the hour with "Mata Hari," and such compulsive electronic games as "Asteroids" and "Space Wars," watching lights light up and hearing bells ping and chime. But this was not to be. Evidently, several men had come to the pinball room on the assumption that they could pick up a girl, and some girls had come here, too, on the same assumption.

"You want a little competition?" said one sidling up to her.

"No," she answered, dropping several more quarters into the machine she was standing in front of.

He would not give up until she told him in no uncertain terms that she wanted him to leave.

Just as he suddenly retreated she observed out of the corner of her eye a familiar figure entering the packed room. Not Teddy. It was Jim Corona. Somehow he had managed to slip by the doorman.

"Oh shit," she muttered to herself, "he followed us, and he's looking for me."

He had abandoned his pirate costume, probably leaving it in his car. There was no question that he was wholly dedicated to finding Martha; he passed half-naked nubile women without blinking an eye. The look on his face was hard and defiant.

For an instant, Martha froze, her only thought was how to escape. The alternative—a confrontation, recriminations, a public scene (even in a place where public scenes assumed a whole new definition)—was unpalatable to her. And then there was Teddy. She did not want to see what would happen if the two of them clashed.

Because Jim was taking his time, studying the face and figure of every woman who materialized in his visual field, Martha was able to slip out just before he caught sight of her. But she knew that he would not abandon his search, that once he got obsessed about something (and he surely seemed to be obsessed about her) he would not give up.

Well, she concluded, there is no choice; the best way to hide is to surrender to the anonymity of the hot tub where she would be surrounded by dozens of others, equally naked, equally submerged in water and steam.

She rented a locker, hurriedly disrobed, and clad only in a towel wrapped as decorously as possible, she sauntered into the public area, hesitated for a moment, then dropped the towel and took the plunge.

Sinking into the burning water was such a shock that Martha felt as though she'd been thrown into an oven. But then her body relaxed, succumbing to heat-induced lassitude. She noticed that her skin was turning pinkish in color. For the moment she forgot about Jim, forgot about Teddy, was aware only of the others who occupied her sector of the tub.

Their nakedness interested but did not arouse her. In her soporific state nothing seemed to matter. Half the night had been spent running about with costumed people, in disguise herself, the other half was apparently to be spent in the company of those without any clothes at all. There was, she thought, kind of a delicious irony in this.

The man who approached her, clinging to the side of the tub as he worked his way around to her, was not bad-looking, with moist black hair tumbling over his brow and eyes that were accustomed to deciphering the mysteries of a woman's face. He reminded Martha of Jim. He had Jim's body and Jim's smile and when he tried to put the make on her he was exactly like Jim.

"You're somebody famous," he said, so carefully apprais-ing her body that she felt suddenly ashamed.

She gave him a nervous laugh. "Somebody famous? Where would you get an idea like that?"

"You're an actress. I've seen you in something. Weren't you at the Mark Taper Forum last year in the *Doll's House?*"

Martha admitted that she was. Flattered that anyone would remember that performance, she fell into conversation with the man, who said that his name was Rick and that he was an out-of-work actor (what else?). She was no longer conscious of her nudity or of his for that matter. When he first suggested going with him back to the room he'd rented to "continue our talk," she balked, saying that she really didn't have the time—she really didn't, maybe just twenty, twenty-five minutes before she had to meet Teddy in the Sun Room—but then she spotted Jim, stalking the area around the tub, looking like a wild beast about to pounce.

"Wait, I've changed my mind," she said. "But I'm warning you I can't stay longer than half an hour."

"No problem," Rick said agreeably.

But once he got her into the room he didn't waste a moment in getting out the cocaine and the amyl nitrite he'd stowed away in his clothes.

"I don't do snow," Martha said, adding a qualification: "As a rule."

"Rules are made to be broken." Rick handed her a slender metal straw. "Why don't you do a couple of lines? Relax."

She was wearing only the towel, and it was obvious that she was in need of relaxation.

With the introduction of the cocaine into her system she no longer felt so apprehensive, and not just of Rick but of Teddy and of Jim. She kept asking Rick for the time, and he continued to assure her that they had plenty of it left and not to worry. She began to suspect that he was deceiving her, but while she told him repeatedly that she would have to go any second now she made no move to do so. And when he reached forward and in one deft movement untied the towel so that it slipped down on her thighs, carelessly draping them, she put up no resistance. All she asked was, "Do you do this all the time?"

"No," he answered, "only Thursdays, Fridays, Saturdays and Sundays, the rest of the week I recover."

All she said was, "I shouldn't be doing this." But whether she meant by "this" that she shouldn't be fucking a man she'd met fifteen minutes before or that there simply wasn't time enough to indulge herself she didn't quite know. It was all very confused in her mind.

He started out gently, aware that she was still a bit jittery, but as she began to respond, he grew more aggressive, dropping his head down into her lap, causing her to assume a supine position on the double bed. With a calculation that could only have come from a great deal of practice, he used his tongue with uncanny precision and little by little he elicited from Martha the responses he wanted, expected, delighting in the way her pelvis lurched, the way her whole body rocked, the way she threw her head back so that her hair was strewn over her eyes, obscuring them from view. This had gone off better than he had hoped. The truth was that he had never seen her on the stage of the Mark Taper, had merely seen an advertisement for the show in the daily *Hollywood Reporter,* but he had a good memory and a better rap so what difference did it make?

Martha gripped his head fiercely with her hands and pulled him suddenly up to her so that their heads abutted. They kissed. He moved into her because he, too, was a little anxious about the time. There were others he wanted to make it with tonight, and he didn't want to let too many opportunities pass him by.

The two were so entangled and so otherwise preoccupied that neither one of them noticed that the door had opened and that someone was there watching them in a manner not unlike that of a zoologist observing a couple of baboons in heat. The expression on his face was one of curiosity and also perhaps one of puzzlement, as though he wasn't exactly sure what to make of it.

Quietly, he shut the door behind him and from out of the satchel he'd brought with him he removed a cleaver. Then, with timing and speed that were remarkable in circumstances others might find somewhat daunting, he sliced off Rick's head at the base of the neck.

The head rolled off Martha, leaving surprisingly little blood behind, and bounced once on the floor before coming to a stop, face up. There was a certain astonishment reflected on that face, Teddy thought, but mostly there was passion. He had not died at a bad time really.

Martha's eyes could not have gotten any wider. The terror that held her in thrall would not permit her to cry out. But for just a brief moment she no longer concerned Teddy. He was still looking at the face of the man he had just decapitated. He realized that he'd erred, that having spotted Jim Corona earlier in the night he had assumed that this was he. Were it only an anonymous male whom Martha would have obliterated from her memory by tomorrow morning that would not have disturbed him. But when he suspected that she had taken up with Jim, right under his very eyes, as it were, well, that had gotten him rather aggravated.

He regretted having to kill Martha. This was not how he had planned the evening, and he had truly meant it when he invited her to accompany him to Acapulco upon the culmination of the shooting.

But there was no getting around it now; decapitating somebody—without provocation yet—was hardly the sort of thing one forgives and forgets.

Though Martha actually bounced from the bed with considerable speed she felt as though she wasn't acting nearly fast enough, that she was imprisoned in a dream in which all movement, both hers and Teddy's, was occurring in slow motion. And even as she grabbed hold of a towel as though it could protect not only her modesty but her imperiled flesh as well, she could not believe that this was happening. It was so far removed from anything in her normal experience, so utterly unprecedented in her life that she still had the feeling that all she'd have to do was open her eyes and it would all disappear. But her eyes were open, of course, and the head of the man who'd just been making love to her was right in the middle of the floor, and his eyes too were open though they were glazing over quickly.

Martha backed away from Teddy but this was not much help since the room was so very small.

Finally, she got out a word, and the word was "No!" delivered in an enfeebled voice. And again: "No, no, no!" Appealing to Teddy, she recognized the futility of prevailing upon him. For the man who faced her now scarcely resembled the man who had charmed and excited her all this time. He was someone deranged, a man who could not be reasoned with the way the Teddy she was acquainted with could.

And while she wanted to scream, she could not bring herself to, fearing that at the instant she alerted anyone outside the door to her plight, Teddy wouldn't hesitate to kill her.

So she did the only thing she could think of to save herself, or at least to stave off the inevitability of death, which was to drop to her knees, a gesture so unexpected that Teddy stared at her in amazement, his cleaver frozen in mid-air. Then, swallowing back the vomit that rose to the back of her throat, she quickly unzipped his fly and drew out his tumescent organ. It was the violence that had made him hard, she thought. And she opened her mouth to receive him, at the same time shutting her eyes, hoping that by distracting him in this manner she might gain a few precious seconds in which to escape.

Teddy arched his back, stiffening as the pleasure began to overwhelm his impatience at getting this whole thing over with. One more time, he was thinking, what difference would it make? He ran a hand through her hair, occasionally pulling hard at it and causing her to cry out even as he continued to work her mouth along the base of his penis. But he retained hold of the cleaver. And then when he felt that he could hold back no longer, he shuddered, releasing himself into her. It was precisely at that instant that Martha drew back and in one agile motion scrambled for the door. Teddy did not move. His eyes popped open, but he did not move. He watched her as she took hold of the handle to the door. It was then that he leaned forward and swung the cleaver so that it collided with her neck.

But because her tangled hair was in the way, and because the blade itself was somewhat blunted from the first beheading, the cleaver failed to achieve the objective Teddy had intended for it.

Instead of a clean cut, which was what Teddy always hoped for, the cleaver penetrated only partway into the neck, and though it severed the spinal cord and was certain to prove fatal eventually, it did not succeed in killing Martha right off.

She screamed, but the sound she produced was so weak that Teddy doubted anyone outside the door could have heard it. Blood gushed from the wound while Teddy struggled to extract the cleaver caught in the bone. And as he did, she was convulsed in pain, grappling at the door as though by escaping out into the corridor she could escape her fate as well.

Failing to free the cleaver so that he could strike again, Teddy decided to apply further pressure so that he would in effect saw through what remained of his victim's neck. In this he enjoyed more success.

Little by little Martha ceased flailing, ceased squirming. Little by little her head with all its lovely hair, now soaked through with blood, came away in Teddy's hand, and at last her body crumpled to the floor.

Teddy awakened to the fact that he could not go out into the public area looking like this, not with so much blood covering him. He thereupon removed his gloves and all his clothes, and these he stuffed into the satchel. Into it also he placed the murder weapon.

The satchel might identify him, he knew, and he could not risk taking it out of the premises. But he had prepared for this eventuality, having brought with him a small alarm clock that came equipped with an ingenious little bomb. He set it to detonate in an hour and a quarter on the assumption that by then the police should have initiated their investigation.

Quickly, peering out of the small gap he made in opening the door, he waited until he was certain the hallway was empty, then hastened out. A few minutes later he had, unobserved, inserted the explosive satchel in a locker that he secured with a combination lock.

Now, with a towel wrapped around his privates, he looked like hundreds of others circulating through the club who appeared more depleted and more desperate given the lateness of the hour. Teddy reasoned that it should not be too difficult to make off with somebody else's clothes: he could not walk out clad only in a towel.

The fit wasn't exactly right, nor the style to his taste, but Teddy had no difficulty finding suitable attire that some man had left lying about while he went off to contribute to the decline of Western civilization.

Not more than ten minutes after Teddy, unnoticed, had left the club, Jim Corona began his exploration of the private rooms, absolutely intent on catching Martha in the act. In doing this he disturbed a number of couples who, while cursing him, did not generally accuse him of being a pervert, that classification having very little meaning in a place like this.

Methodically, Jim went from one room to the other until he got to the room that Martha and Rick occupied. Without knocking, for Jim was never one to stand on ceremony, he threw the door open and looked toward the bed.

What he saw at first confused him—a man's body sprawled in a growing pool of blood that had begun to ooze off the bedsheets and onto the floor. His mind refused to absorb the horror, and he hardly dared look farther. He couldn't help himself though. He stepped into the room, but in doing this found he'd placed his foot on top of something slippery and malleable. Another body, more blood. And then he noticed Rick's head, face up.

He grabbed hold of the door jamb to keep his balance. He felt faint, his vision kept blurring. Staggering back, he retched, but the horrors he had just witnessed were nothing in comparison to what awaited him.

For there, sloppily bundled in a blood-saturated towel, in the middle of the room, not far from where Rick's head lay, was another head. Jim did not have to guess at whose it was. A quick glimpse at the body he'd inadvertently stepped on—and a quick glimpse was all that he could manage—told him that this must be the head that went with it.

Afraid to look, he looked, carefully unfolding the towel so that it fell away, revealing Martha's head, her face wiped free of blood so that there was no doubting who it was.

From a place deep within him, Jim threw his head back and shrieked for all he was worth, a keening sound so penetrating that it could be heard even above the cascading waters of the Jacuzzi, and it just about stopped everybody in their tracks, waylaying even those in the heat of passion.

And then, overcome as much from the noxiously sweet stench of death as from the sheer shock and terror of it all, Jim fainted, toppling over onto a floor smeared with blood so that he, too, looked like he'd been one of the victims.

Chapter Ten

Harry was just getting into bed, pleased that finally he would be rewarded for a long night's work with oblivion, when the phone rang.

Wrong number, he prayed, recognizing that he'd probably exhausted his quota of luck for the day, that it was more likely bad news.

He was not surprised to hear Bressler's voice on the other end.

"We've got trouble, Callahan."

"Is that any surprise?"

"The bastard from the Tocador. . . ."

"What about him?"

"Looks like he struck again. In a sex club on Folsom."

"What's the address?"

Bressler gave it to him. "Hear you got the asshole that might be the Mission Street Knifer."

"That's right. Well, it's obvious he isn't our friend from the Tocador."

"No, no, he isn't." Bressler wasn't willing to concede the possibility he'd been wrong by putting Harry onto the Knifer while the psychopath he really wanted brought in—because a butcher of pretty women is feared far more than a butcher of homeless derelicts—was still running loose. "I'll meet you down there in fifteen minutes. Hope you haven't eaten in the last few hours. I wouldn't want you to lose your dinner."

That gave Harry an idea of what to expect.

No one, except for those properly authorized, was being permitted to enter or leave the club. What looked like a battalion of police officers stood guard at the exits, nervously averting their eyes from the customers, because they might prove too much of a distraction. Everybody had been ordered to remain where they were and perhaps more importantly, *as* they were. That meant that no one undressed could change that state of affairs until the detectives had completed their investigation.

As time went on, people began growing restive, complaining about their constitutional rights, but being as naked as they were, immersed in saunas, hot tubs, or simply each other, their appeals did not carry much weight. They looked like children who'd been caught jerking off by their prying mothers.

Bressler was there to welcome Harry though it wasn't anything Harry especially liked being being welcomed to.

"Two stiffs: a male, about twenty-five, I'd say, a female, maybe of the same age. Female's been identified as Martha Denby."

"The actress?" Harry was brought up short. He recalled the arresting young woman he'd watched run through a scene just the other afternoon. He generally did not allow things like this to bother him. He had a feeling that this might be different.

"You know her?"

"I don't know her, I saw her once—from a distance."

Bressler nodded. He wasn't much interested, being eager to get on with his presentation. "Same M.O. as the Tocador pérp employed. To a point. By that I mean he chopped off the heads but didn't attempt to do the same with the hands.

And he left the heads behind this time. Probably because he panicked, ran out of time. The place is a fucking mess."

"Who found them?"

They were striding through the public area, two clothed men threading their way through a sea of nudity.

"Fellow who knew one of the victims, this Denby, says he's an actor, Jim Corona."

Harry nodded, recalling the name—and the face.

"He a suspect?"

"Make things easier if he was. But no, he fainted dead away. I use the word dead advisedly. Smelling salts brought him around, didn't help the other two."

"He see who did it?"

"I doubt it, but he's not real responsive when you talk to him. Still in shock. Seems he had a thing for this Denby, hasn't adjusted to the fact that somebody lopped off her head. You're going to want to talk to him. And you're going to have to make him come up with something. Because on something like this we'll need all the help we can get."

"What about these other jokers?" Harry surveyed the orgy that had come to an unexpected and brutal halt.

"Oh, we've been questioning them all right, but you got people burning up in the hot tub and you got people fucking their brains out and you think they're going to notice if somebody looks a little suspicious? And on Halloween night when half of them are coming in and going out in costumes? Everything's suspicious, and nobody gives a shit."

Harry had to agree with this assessment. A twenty-four-hour sex club was not the best place to acquire a reliable witness.

"And I presume there are a few people you've got here who'll give us false names and addresses because they'd hate to have their wives find out they've been here."

"That's right, that's exactly the way it is," Bressler said. Down the corridor, off of which were the private rooms, additional police officers were milling about. A balding man, grown too thick in the waist, whom Bressler identified as one of the managers, was heatedly engaged in conversation with a plainclothesman. He was insisting that his operation was legitimate, that this unfortunate "incident" as he kept referring to it, was simply an aberration that should not be allowed to reflect on the club's integrity and adherence to the legal statutes of the city.

"But we are not arguing over your license," the plainclothesman was saying. "We want to find out who did this fucking thing."

With Bressler leading the way, Harry entered the room where all the mayhem had occurred.

"Everything's just the way Corona found it. Haven't found the murder weapon yet. We're still looking."

Harry stooped down so that he could better make out the head of Martha Denby.

"At least the bastard didn't burn the joint down," Bressler added, searching for the silver lining in all of this, probably because he was already rehearsing his story for the mayor tomorrow.

"Fingerprints?" Harry asked, stepping out of the room now because there was just so much that he, even with his hardened stomach, could take.

"We're getting in the forensic guys real soon, but I wouldn't expect much. The blood, you know. Covers over everything." Now he looked coldly at Harry. "I don't care what you have to do. I don't care where you have to go. But you're going to find this creep. It could be your ass, it might very well be mine."

"I understand," Harry kept his voice neutral.

"I don't want to know what you do, I don't want to know about it. You just bring me the creep on a silver platter by the end of next week." He left unsaid what punishment he might mete out if Harry failed, and Harry certainly wasn't about to inquire.

Harry turned to the detective who had been questioning the manager for the last half hour. He was young and very serious, and he gave the impression of someone who believed all cases ultimately could be solved and closed. His name was Shaw, Jerry Shaw.

"I can't get anywhere with him," Shaw said, indicating the bald man who only came up to his shoulder in height.

"Whaddya mean you can't get anywhere with me? I'm telling you true what I know."

Harry drew Shaw aside. "What about the other people here, the customers, the staff? They notice anything?"

"We got a couple of people who seem eager to tell us their life stories, one son of a bitch who invited me to join him in the sauna, but in all this craziness nobody has come up with anything we can use. You know, nothing *reliable.*"

"That's what I figured. Where have you got Corona hiding?"

"Over in that room there." He pointed to a door that was guarded by two of the more imposing officers on the force. "We've been plying him with a couple of shots of whiskey. It may not be in accordance with departmental rules, but Jesus, that guy really needs a drink."

"He needs a lot more than a drink," Harry noted.

As he was about to step away from Shaw, Shaw stopped him.

"Just one question."

"Sure."

"You the Harry they call Dirty Harry?"

"That's right."

The whiskey didn't seem to be doing Corona a whole lot of good. His face was ashen—ghosts don't look any whiter—and his hands were trembling as they clutched the glass containing his restorative.

"Your name is Jim Corona?" Harry maneuvered a chair up to the bed where the man was sitting, listless and inattentive.

The room was, in all its aspects, a duplicate of the one in which Martha and the unidentified lover had met their end. It was an odd transformation that had occurred; an hour ago people had come to this room for sex, now they came for interrogation.

Harry, eliciting no response from the young man, repeated himself, touching his hand in hope that the contact would bestir him.

"Yes," he answered at last. "I've told you people everything I know. I just want to go home and be left alone."

"I understand your feelings perfectly."

This caused Jim to raise his head and regard Harry with bitterness and anger. "How could you understand? Just what makes you think you could understand?"

Calmly, Harry replied, "Because I lost my wife. Because just like Martha, she died suddenly and violently." This was true. A hit-and-run driver had destroyed her and in taking her life, had taken a part of Harry's as well.

Jim had not been expecting anything like this, and it sucked the anger right out of him, leaving only a vast and profound despair. He buried his face in his hands, and his whole body shook with sobbing.

Harry waited for several moments longer. "How did you know Martha would be here tonight?"

"I didn't," he mumbled, his voice hoarse and in danger of petering out altogether. "I didn't. I followed her here. If I'd stopped her from leaving the party. . . ."

"What party was this?"

So Jim explained, and Harry took it all down. "This party, did it have a guest list?"

"I don't know. Yes, I think it did."

"Good, good, we might be getting somewhere. Now Jim, think a minute. Did you see Martha come in here with anybody? You followed her, right? Was she with the victim when she entered the premises?"

"No, no, I don't know who he was, never saw him before

in my life. No, it was with some older dude. I didn't get a good look at him. It was dark, and I kept a good distance away, you know, because I didn't want Martha seeing me."

"Old? How old would you say?"

Jim shrugged. "Middle-aged, fifty, fifty-five maybe, I don't know."

"You get a look at the car he was driving?"

"It was a white Porsche."

"You see the license plate?"

"No, I didn't notice it. I was concentrating so much on Martha I wasn't paying attention to things like that."

"That's all right. You and Martha have been what, lovers, friends?"

"Lovers, I'd guess you'd say."

"How long?"

"A couple of months since the shooting began. I'm working on a movie, you know."

"Yes, I saw you once. You were quite good." Ironically, the scene that Harry remembered witnessing was grimly prophetic of what was to come.

This surprised Jim. "You did, you saw me? In the dog-food commercial on the tube?"

"On the set with Martha just a couple of days ago. Let's say I sort of happened on the shoot. Did you suspect Martha was seeing anyone else? She come to a place like this a lot?"

"Hell, no." Jim was outraged at the suggestion. "She was a homebody. Whoever that asshole was that took her here, he was the corrupting influence. She lives in L.A., she wouldn't know about a place like this."

"But this older man, you think this was somebody else she was seeing? Somebody she might have picked up from the party?"

"Mmmm, let's see. Well, yes as a matter of fact, that was why we were arguing at the party. Yeah, there was somebody else."

"You know who it was, you hear a name?"

"A name? No, I asked friends of mine in the cast, but nobody seemed to know his name. All they said was that she was seeing another guy. Maybe they'll tell you, they wouldn't tell me."

Before Harry could probe Jim Corona further there was an enormous roar, like a thunderclap, but so close that the walls of the room shuddered and Harry was virtually knocked out of his chair. Instantly, smoke floated in under the door.

"Shit, there goes our evidence," Harry muttered.

"What was that?" Corona looked surprised, which was a surprise in itself since he probably had thought he was beyond surprise by this point.

"Stay here, don't move." Harry rushed from the room. The men guarding Corona were coughing from the smoke that seeped along the corridor. They resorted to handkerchiefs, which they put to their noses and mouths.

It was impossible to see more than a foot or two ahead, but Harry could hear all right. People were screaming and yelling, betraying panic and confusion.

After a minute, the smoke cleared, leaving in its wake a toxic, pungent stench that hung tenaciously in the air. Everywhere people were running, oblivious to their partial nudity, oblivious to instructions by police to orchestrate an orderly evacuation. There was always the possibility that there was another bomb cached somewhere that might detonate at any time.

The locker room was in tumult. Half the bank of lockers had been blown to the opposite wall by the force of the explosion, and several other lockers had been ruthlessly torn open, their contents scattered and shredded by the blast.

How many people had died was impossible to determine because everywhere you looked there was a bloody limb or mutilated torso. The victims had just concluded their interviews with detectives and had been allowed to get their clothes and go home. Well, these luckless individuals were never going home.

Others were injured and lay writhing and thrashing about amid the wreckage as policemen hastened to minister to them.

In the rubble somewhere Harry was certain there was evidence crucial to unlocking the mystery of the murderer's identity. But given the magnitude of the destruction the police were unlikely to have much success in sifting it out.

Bressler appeared shortly, and the way he regarded Harry was practically as though he blamed him for this latest disaster.

"You spoke too soon when you said he didn't burn the joint down this time. This joker just doesn't cut and run, he leaves his calling card, too."

Outside they heard the wail of sirens as ambulances and fire trucks came barreling down Folsom.

"You're going to get this bastard, aren't you, Harry," was all that Bressler would say. It was not a question either.

Chapter Eleven

Over the course of the next three days, Harry followed every lead that Corona had provided him with. In doing this, he had as much help as he needed, for apprehending the man who had now struck twice in San Francisco had been given highest priority. Basically, what Harry had to go on was a white Porsche and the invitation list for a costume party given on Union. Everybody who was on that list would have to be interviewed. Every Porsche dealer would have to be asked whether he had ever sold a white Porsche and to whom if it turned out he had. And, of course, anyone sighted in such a car, particularly if he was a middle-aged man, would be placed under surveillance.

Eventually, the white Porsche was found—smashed and burning at the bottom of a steep cliff off Coastal Highway 1, not far from the resort town of Timber Cove. There was no occupant nor was there any witness found who could tell the authorities in Timber Cove how the vehicle came to plummet off the highway.

The invitation list was scarcely more helpful. First, there were hundreds of names on it, and second, the sponsors of the party, Global Film Company executives, admitted that many people had undoubtedly gotten in who were not on the list, friends of friends, enterprising bullshit artists who could talk their way into a private party at the White House if they had to, and so the original list was far from reliable. What's more, Harry realized, he wasn't certain which name he was looking for. It was just at this point that any clue whatsoever would be invaluable.

In the interim, the police lab was working overtime in an effort to sort through all the debris that had been carefully recovered from the floor of the devastated locker room. Like archaeologists picking through pottery shards and metal fragments from a lost civilization, the technicians toiled indefatigably in an effort to separate and identify the various objects. But there were so many of them, and there was so much that had been incinerated in the explosion and the fire that it sparked, that little hope was held for finding anything significant soon—or ever, for that matter.

Frustrated, cursing the murderer's shrewdness in concealing all evidence that might lead police to him, Harry decided that he would take advantage of an offer that had not so long ago been made to him.

Which was why he found himself on the fourth day of November in front of Cavanaugh-Sterling Headquarters.

William Davis, Harry reckoned, would have connections that practically no one else in the city had, and he hoped to take advantage of them. And it wasn't as though Davis was not an interested party. Global, after all, was a subsidiary of his company, and though no public announcement had yet been made, it was obvious that production on the movie being shot in the city would be suspended indefinitely. With one lead actress dead and her male lead confined to a psychiatric hospital for shock, there was no way that the movie could be completed. It would prove too expensive to recast and start all over again.

Although Harry had been assured that he would not have to wait to see Davis, he was not surprised to find himself banished to a waiting room where the only source of distraction were old magazines and the most recent stockholder's report, in which Cavanaugh-Sterling's executives gave themselves a pat on the back for record-high earnings in the previous twelve-month period.

Harry gave Davis five minutes, which was about what he expected Davis would give him if he ever got in to see the man. Then he returned to the secretary, a young woman of nineteen or twenty whose pretty face was tautened into a look of perpetual exasperation. Working for Davis must take years off your life, Harry thought as he stared at her.

"You tell Mr. Davis that I can't wait."

"Please, don't be impatient. Mr. Davis is a very busy man. You don't know." The secretary, as though to convince him, showed him a list of names. "Telephone messages," she said. "Just from this morning."

"I'm impressed. I sympathize. But I'm still leaving."

The secretary panicked and buzzed Davis. After conferring with her boss for a few moments, she ran out to where Harry was waiting for the elevator to come.

"He'll see you now, sir." She took hold of his hand, fearful that he might go away anyhow, then, realizing that this gesture was an inappropriate one for a secretary to make, quickly released it.

Davis seemed no different to Harry than when their last interview had taken place. If anything, he looked better, his skin burnished by a Palm Springs tan, his body made leaner by a strict regimen of exercise and eighteen holes of golf twice weekly.

"Pardon the delay, Inspector, it has been a trying morning." He motioned Harry to sit, adding, "They're all trying mornings. For a man in my position there's no escaping responsibilities, I am afraid."

Harry waited a moment longer to see if he had anything else he wanted to say in his defense, then began himself, "I am sure you've heard about what happened down on Folsom Street three nights ago."

"A terrible tragedy."

"And, of course, it is a tragedy that directly affects you."

Davis looked puzzled. "In what way?"

"In that it has shut down production of one of your subsidiary's films."

"Ah yes, of course. Global. So it has." Davis did not sound disturbed by this, and it was possible that it was the first time he'd given the matter any thought. On the other hand, Harry decided, this man seemed absolutely incapable of expressing any emotional response whatsoever.

"Well, it could be worse," Davis continued after reflecting for a moment. "Movies are a risky business as you know and what with advertising costs, which can double your below-line expenditures, very often you make more by shelving the project altogether."

"Then why go into the business at all, Mr. Davis?"

"Write-offs. The longer I live the more business, all business, I don't care whether it's movies or toilet paper, comes down to just one thing. Write-offs."

"Write-offs?" Harry repeated dubiously.

"That's exactly it." Davis smiled triumphantly as though he had just imparted a great piece of wisdom to his guest.

But tax write-offs were not what Harry had come here to discuss.

"If you don't mind, I'd like to get back to the subject."

"The subject? Ah, you mean the unpleasantness down on Folsom Street?"

"Unpleasantness is one way to put it." Harry made no effort to keep the sarcasm out of his voice. "I would be greatly appreciative if you could use whatever contacts you have in the movie business or out of it that might help us find the killer. All we know at this point is that he is middle-aged and has been known to drive a white Porsche."

"And that's all? I would have thought the police would've made greater progress than that."

"Sometimes these things are a bitch to crack."

The phone began to ring, but Davis ignored it. "Yes, I

realize that. I suppose that I should not maintain very high expectations of the police, present company excepted, of course. I am still waiting for a report pertaining to the identities of the terrorists who attacked the Cavanaugh-Sterling executive staff."

"I can't help you there. I am no longer working on that case."

"It's not of any importance right now. I've bolstered my security force. At least I have the privilege of buying protection. I fear for the citizens of our city who are forced to rely on the police for it. Not that there aren't some brave men among your people, but they operate under the handicap of laws which systematically undermine the rights of the victims for the benefit of the criminals."

Just as he had refused to enter into an argument over taxes, Harry balked at discussing the police force's relationship to the law or the populace. "I must ask you again, Mr. Davis, do you think that you could help me? Perhaps if you communicated to the people who run Global, somebody there might know something. We have fairly reliable information that this middle-aged man—"

"Our Porsche driver?"

"That's right. This man was seeing Martha Denby at least for a few weeks prior to her death."

"Martha Denby?" Davis was looking bewildered again.

"One of the victims. The actress in the film your company was shooting."

"Oh yes, how stupid of me. It's hard to remember these things. Cavanaugh-Sterling owns, completely or at least in part, eighty-seven companies, you realize. Global is just one of them."

"A man of your responsibilities has too much on his mind, I expect."

"That's correct, Inspector."

The phone was demanding to be answered again.

Davis stood up. The interview was obviously at an end. "I will do all in my power to help you find this man. And if anything develops I certainly will notify you immediately."

He took Harry's hand. "It's always good to see you," he said in the manner of a conscientious host at a cocktail party. "You can find your way out?"

"I can always find my way," Harry told him, but Davis wasn't listening. He was already on the phone and for him Harry wasn't there any longer. That was how Davis was, going from one thing to another, one person to the other, never looking back.

The afternoon wasn't a total loss. Owens came by Harry's desk and told him that if he was free he was invited to dinner that evening.

"My wife is worried you're not eating right. She feels responsible for putting some nourishment in your body."

"That's very thoughtful of her. You can tell her that I accept. By the way, how's that shoulder?"

Underneath Owens' shirt Harry could barely make out the white swaths of tape that held the bandages in place. "Recovering nicely. Still hurts if I move too suddenly, but nothing to get alarmed about."

With the slaying of the Mission Street Knifer, or the Halloween Monster as Owens now referred to him, Owens was no longer assigned to Harry who was once again on his own. But even in the short time that they'd been partners, perhaps partly because of what they had gone through together in Golden Gate Park, Harry regarded him as a friend. And in a department, department hell, in a world where people came into Harry's life too fast and left too easily, it was good to be able to hold onto a friendship. It was good to hold onto anything.

And because Owens was his partner no longer, Harry felt relieved, shorn of the burden he'd been carrying around with him since Bressler had united them. He didn't have to be responsible for Owens' life. Only his own and that, God knows, was responsibility enough.

Dinner was to be at seven, right after Harry was due to get off from work (though with this case the work, the plodding routine of the work, never ended, and Harry stopped only when he was too exhausted to stand or focus his eyes). But by the time he arrived at the Owens home, the table was set and Mary Beth was waiting with an open bottle of Spanish red wine.

"I hear you're worried I'm not eating well," Harry teased her as he entered the house.

"Let's just say I'm concerned. From the way Drake talks about you I wonder if you're eating at all."

"If you want to call half a tuna sandwich and a Big Mac eating, well, then I'm eating."

The dinner that Mary Beth had prepared was somewhat more extravagant than half a tuna sandwich and a Big Mac in that it consisted of flounder broiled in a Dijon mustard sauce that gave it a tart yet subtle taste. The only problem was that Harry scarcely had any appetite left, no matter how good the food in front of him.

Owens asked him what was wrong. Although Harry usually made it a point to say nothing about his work on purely social occasions, the mystery of the Tocador murderer weighed so heavily on him that he couldn't help himself. He feared that somewhere out in the city that very evening the man would strike again. What right did he have to be sitting here and enjoying excellent food and company?

So he told Owens and his wife about the case, much of which they already knew from the papers. And, of course, Owens had heard a good many stories that were floating around the department. But neither of them was aware of all the particulars. Without being specific (essentially because he couldn't be specific), the police commissioner had, in a statement to the press, implied that there were significant leads in the case and that while an arrest might not be imminent it could be expected "shortly." The idea behind this reassuring, and rather misleading, declaration was to lessen the growing anxiety of the populace and to bolster the public's perception that the police were actually getting somewhere. A second motivation was the hope that if the perpetrator felt he was in danger, he might panic and do something stupid or just plain clumsy and in that way expose his identity.

Needless to say, from the mayor on down, extraordinary pressure was being applied now to invest the commissioner's words with credibility. If the commissioner stated that there were significant leads well, goddamnit, somebody had better come up with them—and quickly. And being, more or less, at the bottom of this pressure cooker, Harry felt the heat most intensely.

"Now it seems to me," Harry was saying, "we have two interlocking parts of the puzzle. In one part we know the identities of the victims. One is Martha Denby. . . ."

"I'm still shocked that it could happen to such a sweet girl," said Mary Beth who, while never regarding her as sweet in life, felt obliged to defend her honor now that she was dead.

Harry continued. "The other, just identified yesterday, was an out-of-work actor who drove a taxi on weekends. His name is Rick Hollister. That's one-half of one part, that's all we got. We have no trace of the murderer.

"All right, now the other part is even worse. That's the Tocador slayings. In that part we not only don't know who the killer is we don't even know who the victims were. It's been weeks now, and the forensic boys haven't come up with anything that might somehow tell us who those two girls were. We've circulated ads in this part of the state and wired departments in most of the major cities in the country, requesting information on any missing women. And we've been deluged all right, but nothing connects. And no one's stepped forward to claim the bodies. Whoever those girls were, if they've got anybody to cry over them, they're doing it in private.

"Now it is my belief that if we're to make any progress on this thing we have got to have more than one out of four pieces. If we knew who the Tocador girls were, we'd have something to go on."

"How exactly do you mean, Harry?" Owens asked.

"Those girls were not your ordinary ten-dollar hookers, whatever else they were. And the Tocador is not your average sleazy hotel where you've got johns coming in night and day. It's just the opposite, an old-time residential place. So that means the girls were expecting somebody, all right? From what Jim Corona says, Martha probably knew the man who murdered her. Which means that Martha and the Tocador pair probably had one man in common. We find out who the Tocador girls were hanging out with, match it up to somebody who would have access to Martha, and bingo, we might, just might, have our man."

"So you have nothing at all to go on?" Drake persisted.

"What we've got are just a few scraps of clothing, a bit of suede, a bit of velvet, a bit of felt."

Mary Beth looked suddenly fascinated. "How much of each would you say you have?"

Harry shrugged. It had been some time since he'd last examined the evidence. "A few tatters, and they're pretty fragile at that because of the fire."

"I wonder if I could take a look at them."

"I don't see why not. Why are you interested, if I may ask?"

"Well, I know a good deal about clothes. I am a wardrobe consultant—at least I was until they closed down the shooting."

"And Mary Beth worked for a while at a boutique when we lived in L.A."

"I'm convinced. Look, I'd be grateful for anything you can contribute."

"OK, when can I see these tatters? Being unemployed as I am, I have plenty of free time these days. I can do it tomorrow morning if you'd like."

"What about right now?"

"Harry, the lab'll be closed now," Owens pointed out.

"So we'll rouse somebody and make him open up for us."

"Don't you stop for a minute?"

"When the killer stops I'll stop," said Harry and in such a way that Owens was immediately silenced.

It was not so easy to get a man to open up the lab, and when they succeeded more than an hour had passed. A cranky Walter White, armed with a set of keys he jangled in annoyance, greeted them in the hallway directly outside of the lab. He frowned upon seeing Mary Beth.

"She authorized?"

"I'm authorizing her," Harry said.

White looked from her to Harry and back again. Owens he chose to ignore. "Oh, it's one of those, eh?" He decided that he wasn't about to engage Harry in an argument and opening the door, allowed all three to enter.

More time elapsed before White extracted the evidence from a bureau that held large cumbersome drawers. "Somebody fucked up the filing system," he muttered more to himself than to his nocturnal visitors. "Can't find a goddamn thing in all this mess."

But he was being too pessimistic. He knew every nook and cranny and obscure crevice in this lab, and somehow he managed to find things even when they were misplaced or lost.

The shreds of clothing were stretched out on oversized mats and sealed in a plastic container to protect them from further deterioration. Unless you looked closely, one sample resembled the other, each being badly charred and torn.

But extremely brilliant light and magnifying glasses were available, and microscopes, too, if they were required, and in any case, Mary Beth had a practiced eye when it came to clothing. She was able to decipher the original material beneath the black coating even without resorting to the chemical analysis already run by the lab.

"This suede jacket," she said after examining the six mats that had been presented to her. "You see the inside of it there?"

Harry really didn't see it; it all looked equally scorched no matter from which angle the fabric was observed. But he nodded as did Owens who was peering over his wife's shoulder.

"Silver fox fur, I'm almost certain of it. For some reason your people didn't register it in the analysis. Now take this one." She extended a finger toward the next mat. "This is cloche. It's not from a dress or anything like that, it's probably from a hat and I would imagine one of those sculptured antique hats that you rarely see women wearing anymore."

She gazed up at Harry who was growing more impressed as she went on. "Keep going," he urged her. "You're doing fine."

"This third one I'm not sure about. It's suede, but not the same suede as the first fabric I looked at. But this fourth sample, you see the way it curves here. I'd say that what you have here is a kind of pants, knickers, bloomers, something baggy, not my style at all. But it's a very recent thing in fashion, these baggy pants legs for women.

"These last two I can't really say too much about. They're just too far gone, so I guess you'll have to rely on your lab analyses for them."

She turned away from the evidence spread out before her on the table and shrugged almost in apology. "I wish I could do more for you."

"No, no, really, you've been very helpful," Harry assured her.

"You're not just saying that."

"No. All right, all this stuff, what you're saying is that it's the latest in fashion, glamorous, chic? Is that the proper conclusion to draw?"

"Oh yes."

"Could you walk into a department store and buy this junk, you pardon the expression?"

Mary Beth shook her head determinedly. "Oh no. This is specialized, you would probably find these items in a classy boutique."

"Maybe we are getting someplace," Owens said.

Harry looked at him, noting his use of the plural; he seemed to be getting caught up in this case, too.

"But wait, I think the shop you want is a very unique place. Because of this cloche hat, you see."

"How do you mean?"

"If it is antique like I think it is, then it was probably purchased at a store that specializes in accessories as well as highly experimental fashion. And if my guess is right one of these velvet numbers could be antique just like that hat."

"Of course, all these things could have been purchased from different stores," Owens said. "I don't want to spoil the party or anything."

"Yes, that's true," Harry admitted. "What do you think, Mary Beth?"

"I think that most of these things came from one, maybe two shops. These Tocador girls, as you call them, they undoubtedly had a great many clothes at home."

"Wherever home is," Harry added.

"And they could be expected to spend a lot of their time shopping. Which leads me to believe that for the image they wanted to project they very well might have relied on a kind of customer service. There might be a woman or a man, it could be either, who dressed them."

"Like a fashion designer?" Owens suggested.

"I don't think they were models though. Models you find may show off fancy clothes and very fashionable things, but as a rule most of the ones I know dress fairly simply on their own. No, these were girls who liked to costume themselves. At least that's my guess. I could be wrong."

"You could be, yes," Harry said, "but since nobody else has come up with a better theory—in fact, nobody has come up with any theory—I am going to operate on the assumption that you are right, that there is such a store and that if I can find it, somebody there will be able to tell me who the Tocador girls are. A long shot but what the hell?"

"What I suggest you do, Harry, is to go to places like Daljeet's on Haight or Tropics on Market. Or you might try Flora which is somewhere in Fairfax. They're the kind of specialty boutiques that might be able to help you even if they don't carry these exact sort of things."

"You think you could write those names down for me? I would greatly appreciate it."

"No problem." Then she broke out in laughter that had both men looking at her in bewilderment.

"What is it?" her husband asked.

"I'm sorry, I can't help it. It's just the idea of Harry marching from one boutique to another, asking if they sell antique cloche hats and velvet skirts. It strikes me as very funny."

"I'll just think of it as an education. Mary Beth, I owe you a dinner—and a dress."

"Nothing like what these girls wore, please," she said. "I'm just a simple country girl."

"Thank God for that," Owens breathed. "Imagine being married to them?" He gestured to the mats with their charred contents glimmering in the intensity of the light. It was almost as if they had collectively conjured up the two dead women from the remnants of the clothes they'd worn.

"I wonder if somebody was," Harry said. "I wonder if somebody was."

Chapter Twelve

After undertaking an investigation into the nature of places like Hot Chilly, Orpheus, Mom's Apple Grave, Tropics, and East/West Leather, Harry began to feel, in a word, foolish. Each boutique seemed to him more eccentric and more theatrical than the last. Who bought all this weird attire? he kept asking himself. Most of the clothes on exhibit seemed meant for a certain type, which to Harry's mind was a sixteen-year-old girl with a lithe body, tight ass, small breasts, frizzy hair dyed a chilling shade of green or blue, who favored big tinted glasses and chewed gum interminably throughout the day and night.

He supposed he was prejudiced. His work, after all, seldom obliged him to explore the world of fashion, high, low, or retro, and understandably, he was in near total ignorance of the way it operated.

His presence in these shops was immediately noticed by proprietors and customers alike. They did not regard him with suspicion, but they certainly did give him some very curious looks. When he identified himself as a police officer, the salesperson he was addressing acted as though she—most often it was a she—was about to be arrested for some obscure crime she'd committed and then forgotten about. But that was not at all an unusual reaction. Everyone felt guilty about something, and it was Harry's sense that a great many people were only waiting for a man with authority to tap them on the shoulder and announce that their time was up. While most of these individuals, randomly selected, would probably protest and assert their innocence, it was very likely that they would secretly believe the officer justified in making his arrest.

When Harry declared that he was just seeking information, the salesperson would visibly relax, breathe easier, and because she would generally feel, however irrationally, that she had just been let off the hook, she would be far readier to help.

Then, one by one, Harry would draw out of the large manila envelope he carried with him full-color glossies of the half-burned evidence. He would then carefully explain just what he was showing them since to the untutored eye what had once been a suede jacket and a velvet dress and a cloche hat looked indistinguishable from one another.

But despite the good intentions of the boutiques' personnel, nobody could say whether these were the sort of items that they might have at one time sold or whether they had once regularly served two young women who mysteriously no longer shopped there.

After a full day of making the rounds, Harry had begun to feel that he was wasting his time. Still he had a strong, gut-level feeling that there was something to what Mary Beth had told him, that it made sense to continue looking further.

Before abandoning the Polk Street area altogether, he stopped in at the Palace Museum, located at 1546. Aside from carrying a full and exhaustive (perhaps even exhausting) line of designer jeans, the store featured what one guidebook said were "once-loved clothes from the twenties to the forties."

A man whom Harry guessed to be in his twenties stepped forward to help. He stared at Harry for a few moments in something like astonishment. "Don't tell me," he started. "You wish to change your whole image. We had in a man just the other day, he was going through a mid-life crisis, you know, divorcing his wife, leaving his home, his work, his family, throwing it all aside for love."

"A younger woman?"

"No, a younger man. It's hard to keep up."

"I imagine it is. But the fact of the matter is I am not looking to change my image."

The man sighed. "What a shame. You certainly could do with a change."

After a day of touring shops like this, Harry was scarcely in the mood to exchange mindless banter with anyone. He got right down to business, pulling out the glossies with an air of resignation. He did not expect to be rewarded here any more than he'd been in the last dozen boutiques.

But after he had described what he was displaying to the man, it proved to be more enlightening than Harry was prepared for.

"We don't sell exactly this sort of thing in our store, but I am pretty certain that the place you are searching for is Lazlo's."

"Lazlo's?"

"It's a specialty shop, very expensive, exorbitant I should say. I'm told there are people who come from halfway around the world to be outfitted there. It's located in Los Angeles. Maybe Beverly Hills, I'm not sure. But they would certainly have the combination of high fashion and antique clothes and unique accessories you're looking for. And they do have personnel trained to clothe their regular customers. Sometimes they will go to the homes of their clients and outfit them there, sparing them the trouble of turning out in public. You know how some of these celebrities get?"

Harry said that he had an idea and then, thanking the man, left, wondering whether this was the lead he'd been searching for.

He phoned Mary Beth with the news.

"Lazlo's, of course," she said. "How stupid of me not to think of it. I could have saved you a lot of time."

"No problem. Tell me, do you think a phone call to them would help?"

"I have the feeling, Harry, that Lazlo—and there is a real Lazlo, some doddering European who claims to have aristocratic lineage, I'm told—acts like he's psychiatrist and father-confessor rolled into one, and he is very scrupulous about protecting his customers. He fears that some newsman will leak word of a star's new fall wardrobe. I know it sounds foolish, but that's the way some of the people in this business are."

"Then I suppose I'll just have to go to L.A. and present myself in person."

"I'm sure you'll be very persuasive."

There was no question of Bressler authorizing the excursion to L.A. He had, for once, given Harry virtual *carte blanche* (though this latitude on his part could scarcely be expected to persist beyond this case). He might very well have authorized a trip to Hong Kong if it would have helped.

But what Harry did not anticipate was Bressler's insistence that he not go by himself.

"Who is stuck with me this time?"

"The same man who was stuck with you last time," Bressler told him.

This astounded Harry. "Why? Have you informed Drake of this?"

"Informed?" Bressler looked mildly surprised as he sat there, tilting slightly in his seat. "I thought you knew. It was Owens who pleaded with me to let him join you. And since you seem to work so well together, after bringing down that monster in Golden Gate, I figured why not?"

Harry realized it was pointless to argue with Bressler, but he did his best to talk Owens out of it. Just as he had been beginning to feel relieved of the burden of guilt that went with having a partner, particularly a partner he liked, that burden had been reimposed.

But Owens was insistent. "I know Los Angeles, I lived there for years, I have contacts there. And besides, we might walk into Lazlo's and find out nothing, just a dead end. That'll be it. It'll be like a small vacation. There's almost no chance of trouble."

"You haven't been around me long enough," Harry said, interrupting him.

"What I was about to say was that if there is trouble I want to be with you. I feel like we, that is my wife and myself, have a stake in this case. If it weren't for Mary Beth you wouldn't even be going to L.A."

His reasoning was not out of line, Harry recognized, but it was Owens' sheer tenacity that convinced him to acquiesce.

He glanced at his watch. They were seated in the living room of Owens' rambling house. It was approaching three in the afternoon. "You know somebody we can stay with there?"

"I surely do. An uncle of Mary Beth, retired film producer, used to be pretty big in the business years ago. His wife died, his kids have all gone off, so he has a lot of extra room."

"Well, call him right now, say that we're coming down there today. Then let's get out to the airport and catch a shuttle."

Within 463.7 square miles there exist eighty-one cities, which together constitute Los Angeles. And in that vast dominion there are six hundred movie and television firms. And in that vast dominion, too, there are more than five million registered vehicles.

And it seemed to Harry and Owens as they drove their rented Ford Matador from the airport into the city that all of those five million vehicles were on the road. Specifically, the road they were taking. It was rush hour, though that phrase carries the rather erroneous implication that a rush is in progress. On the contrary, the freeway system that defined Los Angeles County almost as much as it crisscrossed it had been turned into what New York refugees might call a gridlock. Nothing was moving, and nothing looked like it was going to move any time soon.

As the sun sank lower, the sky, filled with a thick haze to begin with, began to pale, growing not darker but yellower with dust and smog and smoke from brush fires that were erupting on the hillsides with perilous frequency, turning million-dollar houses into burnt-out shells and causing scrub pine and chapparal and sumac to disappear while at the same time releasing their respective odors and dispatching them throughout the city.

The radio was filled with reports about the fires in Sunland, in the Verdugo Hills, and in Carbon Canyon to the east, and the blaze that was running out of control near Lake Elsinore and the one that almost wiped out all of exclusive Country Club Drive.

Harry shut the radio off. He'd had enough news about doom, both impending doom and doom that was already here. After all, he had only to open the windows of the car to discover that there were fires raging on the outskirts of L.A. He didn't need a news commentator telling him about it, too.

"It gets like this this time of year," Owens said with the air of a man who feels obliged to apologize for a home that is in a constant state of disrepair. "The winds, and then there's the dryness. But usually it's not so bad."

Harry and Owens had packed light suitcases on the premise that they wouldn't be staying in L.A. longer than a day or two. Harry, who rarely got to L.A. and even less frequently felt the urge to, hoped that they could find out all they needed and leave by tomorrow. That is if they could ever get off this damn freeway. "At this rate, we could walk and be there faster," he commented ruefully.

"Just hold on. We're beginning to move."

They nosed ahead to the next light. Not far.

"Some move," noted Harry who then lapsed into a sullen silence that did not end until the traffic jam did.

As it turned out, Lazlo's, which was their first stop even before putting in at Mary Beth's uncle's house, was in Beverly Hills, just as the man at the Palace had thought. It was to be found on Melrose Avenue, between La Cienega and Robertson boulevards. This was a predictable location since there were well over a hundred boutiques and antique stores crowded into the same stretch of Melrose. Many of the shops Harry noticed were converted bungalows, testifying to the onetime residential character of the street.

Lazlo's, in size and in elaborateness dwarfed its competitors. The interior was filled with silver latticework and mirrors and tiled floors that brightly reflected the patrons who walked on them. Fountains, partially shielded from view by an enormous profusion of plants and tendril-like growths inching their way up marble columns, sputtered constantly with recycled water.

But the effect was neither warm nor welcoming but rather cold, almost severe, as though the place were designed by some of the same people who put together sets for sci-fi movies. Women who might be customers or mannequins, it was hard to tell which, sauntered from one display to the other, casting indifferent looks at the dresses, jackets, coats, handbags, hats, blouses, underthings, overthings, and jewelry almost as though nothing in the world, be it person or object, could interest them at all.

It required considerable skill to locate somebody who was responsible for more than one department (cosmetics, say, or the exclusive Yendi forties collection). Eventually they were guided to an office where the Matisse and Klee and de Koonings that hung on the walls were not prints but very much originals.

A matronly woman, with hair that looked like one of the traditional wigs British judges wear in court, rose to greet them.

"You are policemen," she said, mulling over the implications of this. "From San Francisco?"

Owens explained why they had come. He then proffered the

glossies that Harry had taken on his rounds of San Francisco boutiques.

The woman, whose name was Ms. Weil (or so it said on the small sign on her desk), shook her head when she saw them. "Such destructiveness," she muttered.

Harry assumed she was referring to the clothes and not to the women who'd worn them. Owens leaned forward to point out to her what each charred shred of cloth represented. He had undertaken the role of spokesman because Harry had wanted it that way. Being more impatient and more irritable than Owens, particularly after their tortuous ride into L.A., Harry had the feeling he would say something, even an innocent remark, that would offend this proper lady, which was the last thing he wanted to do—at least until they obtained the information they wanted from her.

"Is it possible that these items might have been purchased in your store?" Owens asked with the deference he thought appropriate to Ms. Weil's exalted station.

She shook her head. "I don't know." She scrutinized the prints again. "We do stock such apparel as you mention." She was being as noncommittal as possible within the limits of the truth.

"Do you keep a list of your regular clients?"

"We do."

"Would it be possible to examine that list and to have a look at the sales receipts going back say, three or four months?"

"We could never allow that."

Harry could no longer remain silent. "And why not?"

"As a private company we are under no such obligation."

"You could be subpoenaed for your records, you realize," said Owens.

"I suppose that it is conceivable."

"Tell me," Harry said, "is Lazlo here?"

Ms. Weil was evidently unaccustomed to having her employer referred to in such a casual manner. "Mr. Lazlo is out of the country."

"Good for him." Harry smiled politely. Owens didn't like it. The smile was too polite. That wasn't Harry. "Tell me, Ms. Weil, do you keep your records in this office?"

Without considering the reason he'd asked this question, she replied in the affirmative.

"Then would you do us the favor of bringing them out?"

"But I just told you that I cannot do such a thing."

"And I heard you very well. But frankly, your opinion doesn't interest me." He stood up and approached the desk so that he loomed over the diminutive Ms. Weil. "There is a murderer running around San Francisco who so far has been responsible for twelve deaths. He's beheaded a few, blown up a few more, and incinerated the rest in fires he's set. Now, to tell you the truth, it would take us some time to get a subpoena from a judge here, but we'd damn well do it and you know it. And that would just waste time. And I don't have time. My partner doesn't have the time. Only the killer has the time."

Ms. Weil was obstinate in her refusal. "Out of the question. I am certain you have worthy motives but—"

Harry refused to allow her to finish. "Look, I am not interested in hearing excuses—"

The phone rang, and Ms. Weil answered it with relief, thinking that she could terminate this unpleasant discussion by simply ignoring Harry and Owens.

"Ms. Weil," she said to whomever was on the other end.

She didn't get much farther because Harry with one quick and determined motion tore the cord out of the wall, immediately severing the connection.

Shocked, Ms. Weil raised her eyes to Harry, her face flushed, her hands shaking in outrage. "How dare you do that? You are acting illegally, sir, I forbid it."

"Lady, I don't give a shit what you do or do not forbid."

"Harry . . ." Owens started to say because he was genuinely alarmed at what his partner might do. But Harry ignored him.

He chose instead to knock all the papers and the disconnected telephone off her desk. The telephone jangled as it met the floor.

"If you do not bring me those records and all the sales receipts my partner requested just now we are going to systematically ransack this office until we find them. Do you understand me?"

Ms. Weil might have understood, but she was having none of it.

"Well, I never. . . . This is the sort of behavior I would have expected from hoodlums, but police!" She rose from her chair with the evident objective of going for the door.

Firmly, but taking care not to hurt the woman, Harry laid his hand to her shoulder and forced her back to the seat. "We can remain here all night if you prefer, same difference to me." He signaled Owens who took the cue and locked the door in back of him.

It had now begun to register on Ms. Weil that these men were serious and that she would be temporarily obliged to accommodate herself to their demands.

"Very well," she said, "I will get you what you want. But I must warn you that I will report you, and I expect to have you both brought up on charges."

Harry was used to this sort of thing. Owens, however, was not and from the look on his face you could tell that he was quite apprehensive about the consequences of what they were doing. Well, Bressler had given him free rein. He was only taking advantage of his unaccustomed freedom.

Once Ms. Weil had produced the pertinent records, she seated herself in her chair, her arms folded sternly under her heavy breasts, fixing the two invaders with an icy stare. She reminded Harry of a third-grade teacher watching two of her recalcitrant pupils misbehave while she contemplated what sort of punishment she should mete out to them.

"You wouldn't want to help us, would you?" Harry asked her, and when she defiantly shook her head, he gave her a broad grin and said, "I didn't think so."

The idea in sifting through these records was to locate two women who came in often, perhaps once or twice a week, and who bought velvet dresses and suede jackets with silver fox lining and antique cloche hats and to match their names up against all the sales receipts from the last few months. It was Harry's hope that sometime, just shortly before the Tocador Hotel slayings, no additional receipts would turn up to be matched against their names.

It took one and a half hours before they discovered their most likely candidates: Eloise Cummings and Patience Bell. They were frequent and extravagant customers from all appearances. In July they had made purchases totaling three thousand, four hundred and thirty dollars. In August they had made purchases in excess of two thousand, and three times in September they squandered at least a thousand dollars on each occasion. The last date recorded was September 28. One thing in particular struck Harry: they always shopped together. At no time did just Eloise or Patience come into Lazlo's on her own. Real togetherness, Harry thought.

"How were these purchases paid for?" he asked the disapproving Ms. Weil.

Her sharp eyes rested for a moment on the documentation.

"In cash. Always in cash." She had decided that she would cooperate at least to this extent.

"That's a lot of money to be carrying around in your purse."

"We do not question our customers' spending habits."

"No, I imagine not."

"Well," Harry said to Owens, "I think we struck pay dirt." He turned back to Ms. Weil. "Do you know these women?"

Reluctantly, Ms. Weil admitted that she did. "I am acquainted with all of our regular clientele."

"Were they young, middle-aged, old, what?"

"Young. Very young."

"Compared to what?"

A glimmer of a smile came to her lips. "To me. Compared to me. They were frivolous but very spirited. I will say no more."

"Thank you, Ms. Weil. You have been a great help."

After taking down the address of the two women—for they lived together it seemed—Harry and Owens left the woman in peace.

"We'll have to send her a dozen roses," Harry said, a suggestion that astounded Owens.

"She's likely to have us busted."

"I don't think so. I think she rather enjoyed the experience. Send her a dozen roses and a note expressing our gratitude and apologies for disrupting her day. See if anything happens."

Owens shrugged. "It's worth a try, I suppose. Where to now?"

The sun was down by this point, and the night sky was violently red as it mirrored the brush fires running out of control. The air was suffused with particles of dust and soot that got into the lungs and caused people to cough continuously as they hastened to their cars or into buildings because everybody wanted to be somewhere inside.

"We're going to Santa Monica, to visit Patience and Eloise. Or at least to see where they lived."

Robertson Boulevard led into Santa Monica, and with the rush hour over they managed to reach their destination in fifteen minutes.

The two women resided on Ocean, not far from where it intersected with Pico Boulevard. The lights from the nearby Royal Inn were visible even with the dense pollution, but they seemed to be distant and very diffuse.

Across the street Harry and Owens could just make out the gradual slope of the beach, and they could hear, but not really see, the Pacific lapping against the shoreline.

The house they were searching for was typical of many in the area: a white stucco two-story structure with a balcony protruding out from the second floor, from which the people who lived inside could observe the ocean. That was only in theory; it was a wonder that anyone could see more than a few feet away in this atmosphere.

The windows were dark. There was no sign of life. Harry and Owens stepped up to the door. Rang the bell. They heard chimes in response, but no one came to find out who they were.

Harry tried the door. Locked. He suggested they go around to the back. A small cobblestone lane described a semicircle which culminated at a rear door, which also proved to be locked.

"We break in?" Owens asked who was getting better at reading Harry's mind.

"That's right."

"I don't know, Harry. First you intimidate some poor woman and tear out her telephone, now you illegally break and enter a house two women live in who may or may not be dead."

Owens seemed more to be cataloguing Harry's offenses against the state than objecting to them.

"Only one way to find out, isn't there?"

Though he could always employ his .44, which would surely debilitate a lock for good, Harry was more dexterous than that. A credit card was more effective and more—discreet.

Harry used a flashlight. To put on the lights might only alert a vigilant neighbor who'd be inclined to call the police. The very last thing Harry wanted was to face questions from his counterparts on the LAPD.

It was apparent at the outset that Eloise and Patience lived in style. The rugs they had were nearly as deep as the water near the shore, and the furnishings that the narrow light disclosed had that polished, modern look more frequently encountered in the pages of *House Beautiful* than in real life.

Harry touched his fingers to the surface of a chrome-lined glass table and then raised them to his eyes. A coating of dust stained his fingertips. "One would think that if they'd been here recently they'd have cleaned. They seem like the sort who'd maintain a neat house, wouldn't you say?"

And it was true. From what they could see everything was properly in place. Even the plants; they were right where they should be, perched on the windowsills, waiting for the sun to shine through though that might be a long wait and would, in any case, do them no good since just about all of them had died. When Harry touched the leaves of the philodendron plant nearest him they crumbled in his hand.

They discovered a closet. Actually, they discovered a great many closets. There were closets nearly as spacious as some of the rooms, and they were crowded with so many coats, camisoles, kimonos, maillots, bikinis, halters, dresses, pants, blouses, designer jeans and lamé shorts that Harry doubted whether their owners could have worn the same thing twice.

"These girls were really freaks," Owens said, whistling in wonderment at the spectacle.

But what really interested Harry was the prospect of locating a desk, even a drawer where there might be papers, perhaps a journal or diary that would name a suspect.

The girls who lived here, however, seemed to keep little in the way of writing. There were only a few cookbooks, a diet book or two, and many many fashion magazines. They did find a calendar, one of those big-date calendars with a full-color photograph of a Gila monster, the endangered species, it said, for the month of October. (The whole calendar from the Audubon Society was filled with pictures of endangered species.) It was hanging on the wall of the refrigerator and right in the middle of it, in the box labeled 17, was the single name Teddy. October 17th was the day the two women had been killed at the Tocador Hotel.

Teddy, Harry thought. He rummaged in his mind for a corresponding memory, waited for a bell to ring. But there was no memory or bell.

"We have to keep looking," Harry said. "We have to find something else, a letter maybe that could give us more of a clue. Particularly if there are any references to Teddy."

"Teddy," repeated Owens, but his mind was on something else. He began to sniff at the air. "Do you smell something? Smoke?"

Harry's nostrils quivered. "Yes, I do. It's coming from somewhere in the house."

Suddenly there was the sound of glass shattering in the rear of the house. But when the two men sought to find out what had caused it, they were greeted with a surge of flames traveling at an astonishing rate through the whole back of the house. Through the smoke and fire Harry detected the faint but unmistakable odor of gas. He knew, without seeing, what the glass breaking had meant. Somebody had just hurled in some incendiary device to exacerbate the fire that he'd already set while Harry and Owens were investigating the premises on the second floor.

They started to make their way to the front of the house in hope of escaping, but another blaze had started up there. While it was not as fierce as the one in back, it would be soon.

Wherever Owens and Harry went, the flames, like an impassioned predator, followed them, scorching their faces, their hands, singeing their clothing. Worse was the heat, which grew increasingly more intense, gripping hold of the air and sucking the oxygen right out of it. And the smoke, dense and sulfurous, curled thickly through the rooms, obscuring their vision, causing them to sputter and nearly choke as they fought their way to freedom.

The inner structure of the house was surprisingly frail, and though they could not always see its destruction, they could certainly hear it. Wooden beams in the upstairs were giving way, crashing to the floor as their moorings disintegrated. Glass kept exploding as the heat worsened, and just about all the windows in the second-story rooms were obliterated. At the same time, the blaze consumed the vast wardrobe that Eloise and Patience had amassed for a small fortune, the closets affording no protection at all. As the collection of dresses, kimonos, shorts, bathing suits, jackets, and blouses burned, they emitted a strange, almost perfumey odor that mixed with the smoke and the gas.

The rug that was so thick and welcoming to naked feet was more welcoming still to the flames that took root in its tangled fibers and in minutes overwhelmed its surface, then leaped up to the walls, finding further refuge there. The whole house, in fact, even without the gas, was in its chemistry a hospitable environment for the fire.

With their jackets held up over their heads, Harry and Owens, having no other choice, propelled themselves through the fire, ignoring the flames that stung their ankles and the burning embers that bombarded them and the smoke that seeped into their lungs.

The door, either door, in front or in back, was impossible to open. The fire was simply too daunting and the metal knobs of the door handles too hot to risk touching.

So Harry decided that he would simply have to throw himself through one of the downstairs windows that remained intact. He had to jump over a couch directly beneath the window. The couch, like every other article of furniture in the room, was becoming reduced to charred rubble and ash. The fire was in love with the synthetic composition of the couch, and periodically there would be a loud pop as the cushions, of which there were a great many, exploded and released their stuffing.

Harry executed the jump with relative success though this

did not mean he escaped the flames altogether as they danced around his legs. But ignoring the pain, with one foot balanced on the edge of the windowsill, which was sufficiently wide, and with his hands flat against the achingly hot walls for purchase, he kicked at the windowpane with as much force as he could summon. The glass cracked but did not give way. He struck out again, and again the glass shivered and cracked but refused to yield. A third time he tried, and this time the pane shattered, scattering shards all over the place, some of which pincered his legs and arms, penetrating through the cloth like tiny daggers. Then, without hesitation, he threw himself out through the opening he had created though this meant sustaining several smaller cuts as the remaining glass grazed his body in its clumsy passage. He tumbled out in a column of brackish smoke and fell into the shrubbery that grew in front of the house.

Owens, duplicating Harry's movements, leapt to the windowsill and similarly jettisoned himself. Though he thought to roll, to blunt the impact of his fall, he could not quite accomplish this with the shrubbery in the way, and he ended up spraining his ankle.

Harry gathered him up and helped him out toward the sidewalk before the fire could overtake them. Their skin was blackened and crisscrossed by cuts, each of which oozed fresh blood, and their clothes were torn and blackened as well. Harry's brows had been singed, Owens' nearly burned off. From the sky, ash and embers rained down on them.

Only now could they hear the familiar sound of fire engines barreling down Ocean and Pico and Main. Harry suspected that it had taken all this time for the fire department to respond to this emergency because of the scarcity of men and equipment. With so many brush fires needing to be fought around the city it was likely that Santa Monica, along with other communities, had volunteered its firefighters, leaving its department depleted. Undoubtedly, the arsonist had had the same thought when he'd torched the house.

Turning back to see just how extensive the damage was, Harry observed that the house once belonging to Eloise and Patience was going to be a charred hulk. Bright orange flames, with a brilliant blue at their core, sprouted in every naked window of the facade.

"Well, if there was evidence in there, we've lost it now," Harry muttered. "All we've got is Teddy on the 17th. How much is that?"

Owens didn't hear him, concentrating instead on staunching some of his bleeding with a handkerchief he'd managed to dig out of his pocket.

Despite the spectacles they presented, blackened, coated with ash, bleeding from a dozen different locations on their bodies, neither Harry nor Owens was seriously hurt, though Owens felt somewhat embarrassed about going out into the world lacking eyebrows. (For which reason he, with his genius at makeup, gave himself artificial ones that would have to do until the hair grew back.) They were each given emergency treatment when they appeared at a neighboring hospital because it was assumed by the way they looked that their injuries must be serious and worthy of immediate attention. The doctors who ministered to them, residents on night call and still learning their trade for the most part, seemed a bit disappointed to learn the truth. It was almost as if they felt cheated. The way they regarded Harry and Owens they might have thought themselves victims of a grand deception. For the truth was that soap and water and disinfectant, combined with a little suturing and some Band-Aids, were all the men truly needed.

And one more thing: rest.

Chapter Thirteen

When Harry and Owens turned up at Mary Beth's uncle's place—a comfortable and unprepossessing home, with architecture vaguely suggestive of Mexico, set among the streets that snake through Laurel Canyon—they looked somewhat more presentable but still a mess. Their host, McKinley Ninn, a man getting on toward seventy but in no hurry to arrive, failed for an instant to recognize Owens and was almost ready to slam the door in his face until Owens spoke up and identified himself.

Ninn frowned and scrutinized Owens with an eye to determining his true identity. "You sure this isn't another one of your disguises?"

"No disguise, Mac," Owens said, referring to him just as his wife did. "We had a little adventure on the way over." He introduced Harry.

Ninn took Harry's hand and motioned them in. "What you fellows need is a drink. No, let me modify that statement. What you need is a number of drinks."

"And food," Owens said. "Haven't had anything to eat since lunch on the Air West flight we took."

"I'll put some steaks on the stove. No problem."

Since his wife had died and his children gone away to school and to their respective careers, Ninn had lived alone, surrounded by memories frozen in time in the many photographs and posters from old movies that covered virtually all the walls in the house. And while his television was constantly on, and could be said to be his only companion, he seldom bothered to watch it. "I think of it the way I do wallpaper," he said, gesturing to it. "I wait for the late night movies, the good ones, what Howard Hawks and Frank Capra used to do. Those people knew how to make movies. The ones working today, bah!" He snorted in disgust.

Harry imagined that this was the sort of set speech he gave to everyone who entered his house, regardless of how many times they'd heard it before.

The steaks were good and the drinks restorative but exhaustion soon set in as the hour got past eleven. Harry and his partner managed to stay awake long enough to watch the final news broadcast of the evening come on, though what they saw was only a repetition of what they had gone through earlier: fire flickered on the 21-inch screen and, because one blaze resembles another in the way it progresses and in the destruction it causes, the only way they could tell that it was Sunland going up and not Carbon Canyon was by listening attentively to the commentator's voice. Because of the gravity with which these brush fires were viewed (twenty-five-million dollars estimated worth of damages and at least three deaths credited to them), the fire that had devastated the house on Ocean Boulevard hardly rated a mention. It was not even accorded the importance of a still photo, let alone a video spot, perhaps because it was reasoned that there was just so much the public could stand of fires. The commentator, a blandly handsome man with an airbrush hairdo, did state that arson was suspected and that detectives from the arson squad could be expected to investigate. The implication was that they would do this only when they could get around to it, for several of the brush fires were also suspect and there were only so many detectives to go around.

"Tomorrow we go back to Santa Monica and talk to some of the neighbors," Harry told Owens.

"You think any of them are going to talk after what happened there tonight?"

Harry shrugged. "Let's just hope so."

Ninn showed the two men to their rooms. "You get Hank's," Ninn told Harry. "He's my oldest. And Drake gets Tommy's. That's the middle one. Went off to M.I.T., Tommy did, then dropped out and now does medical illustrations for some company in New York. Strange how your kids turn out."

Harry had the feeling that Ninn would have gone on discussing his absent family and his life as a producer in Hollywood had they not cut him short, very politely of course, and said good-night.

"Poor Mac seldom has anyone to talk to," Owens said when Ninn had gone downstairs to continue reading and waiting for a decent movie to come on the air.

"That's all right," Harry said. "Anyone who makes a drink as generous as he does can be easily forgiven. I will see you in the morning."

Harry closed the door, and quickly getting out of his tattered clothes that he hadn't bothered to change before, he dropped on the bed and was out like a light.

In the living room downstairs McKinley Ninn was busy changing the channels until he found a Hitchcock movie from the forties that he'd already seen at least four times. No matter, he settled himself back with a bourbon adulterated only by some slender chunks of ice, prepared to be pleased all over again.

From time to time he would doze off but then would come awake again, usually during a commercial break. But he had no difficulty figuring out what had happened while he'd been unconscious; he had the plot firmly memorized.

Close to one-fifteen he fell asleep for a longer interlude than usual because when he opened his eyes again it was almost two and the movie was in its last, climactic scene. He leaned forward, in a slightly uncomfortable position so that he would not drift off so easily again. He did not want to miss the ending, no matter that he knew it by heart.

And it was because he concentrated so much attention on the television set that he failed to hear the slight noise that came from behind him.

The man who now stood directly behind Ninn's chair was accustomed to silence. He looked like someone who had been entrusted with a great many secrets in his time. His face was a cipher, a blank. His body was thin, pared down, wiry and short like the body of a jockey. In one hand he gripped what in the country of Colombia they call a chonta, a dowel-like instrument used by Indians.

With the practiced movement of a professional, he reached out with his free hand, and, grabbing Ninn under his jaw, he managed to clamp his mouth shut. For a man so small and thin his hands possessed an astonishing strength. In an instant he had succeeded in hoisting Ninn partway out of his chair. Ninn was so taken by surprise that he was incapable of reacting quickly enough.

For his assailant wasted no time. Having neither a conscience nor a mind that carefully weighs moral choices, he never hesitated in the performance of his unusual task. He took his chonta and thrust it decisively into the exposed neck and drew it down Ninn's chest, easily ripping apart his shirt and no less easily his skin and the muscle and organs that lay beneath, gutting him as he would a newly caught fish.

Ninn's body convulsed with the sudden trauma but in less than a minute ceased its resistance. The chonta had perforated so much that was vital and released such grievous hemorrhaging that there was no question of Ninn's surviving past the ending of the Hitchcock film, which was concluding on the set.

The assassin surrendered his hold on Ninn, it no longer being essential, and Ninn with the quiet and grace that had characterized his life slipped back into his chair, his head crumbling to his bloodied chest.

Now the man wiped the chonta against a curtain, cleaning it of the blood and glutinous viscera that had accumulated along its shaft. Satisfied that he had it restored to its original pristine condition, he began up the stairs. He took the additional precaution of a 9mm Short, a handy gun easily contained in the pocket, with push-button magazine release, a fully adjustable target sight, and a seven-round magazine.

Harry awakened, and he came awake with such suddenness that at first he was disoriented. Lying in this strange bed, observing the shape his shadow took on the ceiling, he wondered where in hell he was. He felt like shit, his body belatedly remembering the ordeal he'd been through: the burns, the scrapes, the swelling bruises all began crying out for attention.

Then it occurred to him just where he was and what his situation was, and he decided that it should all wait until morning before he seriously considered what his next step should be. But sleep wasn't anxious to come back to him. He was too fully awake. His mind was filled with just one thing: Teddy on the 17th. His only clue, and it did not seem to lead anywhere. He regretted being deprived of an opportunity to explore the house further, for he was certain the evidence he was seeking must have been there. Or why else would somebody—the mysterious Teddy perhaps?—burn it to the ground? And how had it come about that he and Owens were followed? How had the murderer discovered that they were on their way to Los Angeles?

Distantly, he heard footsteps, scarcely audible against the carpeted staircase. He assumed that it was Ninn finally making his way to bed. But there was another sound, one so low that he had not been conscious of it before. He realized it was the television set, still going downstairs. Then presumably Ninn was retiring for the night; perhaps it was the bathroom at the head of the stairs he wanted. But no, that made little sense, since Harry recalled using a bathroom downstairs.

And because he was of a suspicious nature to begin with, and because something did not *feel* right to him, though if asked to say what it was he would not be able to articulate it, he quietly climbed out of his bed and, still in his underwear, unsheathed his .44 and slipped up to the door of the room and pressed his ear against it, listening.

The man on the stairs stopped, not because he was aware that he might have been heard—on the contrary, he was certain he had not—but because he was deciding which of the two rooms closed to him he should investigate first. After a moment, he made his choice and attaining the landing, advanced directly to the room Owens occupied.

Again he did not hesitate, opening the door so quickly that the hinges did not squeak or offer more than the most muffled sound that Owens, sleeping much more deeply than Harry had been, did not register.

This man, this cipher, had eyes that were sharp, better than 20/20, and his night vision was acute, which made him all the more valuable to those who employed him. He could discern his target, his victim, in the bed, distinguish his form from the shadows and darkness that abounded in the room. Preferring silence as a matter of course and because he did not wish to alert his other intended victim to his presence, he crept up to the bed, which was positioned against the rear wall, and then, when he reached it, stood for just an instant staring at Owens, who still had not stirred. He was enjoying the power he had, and was now about to use, over those who were helpless to resist him or even to realize that their lives were in jeopardy.

Harry, so close to the door of his own room, distinctly heard Owens' door being opened. He listened further but could hear nothing more. Nonetheless, he clutched hold of the doorknob and very carefully, very carefully, twisted it and gradually drew open the door until he had a crack from which to peer out into the hallway. But all he could see was what his ears had just told him—that the door to Owens' room had been opened. Otherwise just darkness.

He decided to step out into the hall, though he could not help but produce enough sound to warn the assassin that he no longer could hope to complete his work in peace. Because the assassin was temporarily distracted, he did not immediately plunge the chonta into Owens but turned to see where this sound had originated.

He caught sight of Harry perhaps an instant before Harry caught sight of him. And in that instant he fired. Though the bullet went way wide of its mark, it did wake Owens.

When Harry returned the fire, a wall mirror hanging over the bed exploded into thousands of fragments, which flew into the air before clattering down to the floor. Both Owens and the assassin sustained minor injuries as glass pinched their flesh.

Owens reacted with commendable speed, jumping out of bed and rolling under it since he had no other option. His gun was way over on the far side of the room.

The assassin, angered that he had lost one man, at least for the moment, without getting the other one, sank into a crouch and fired again. And again, though Harry had darted to the other side of the exposed doorway, out of his sight.

It was then that he turned his attention to the bed, thinking irrationally that Owens would somehow still be there. When he saw that he was gone he was a bit confused as though Owens had pulled a Houdini-like disappearing act. But then the assassin quickly realized his error and understood that there was no place else but under the bed that Owens could be. He risked a second to peer down and see, lowering his gun before his eyes.

Owens watched him as he did this and recognized that there was no way he could get out of his line of fire in time. So Owens did the exact opposite, the most unexpected thing—he crawled toward him and confronted him head-on.

Right then, Harry, crouched behind the protective wall, allowed his head to protrude out enough so that he could see into the bedroom and seeing, fired.

The assassin was looking right into Owens' eyes when the .44 went off. Though the man's gun was virtually at Owens' temple, he was so astonished to see his would-be victim at such proximity that he did something he had not in his entire career ever done—hesitate a moment too long.

The round from the .44 took the assassin in his back, shattering his spine and toppling him over so that he sprawled on the floor in a bed of broken mirror glass. Still, he was alive and moving and had not lost hold of his gun, which he fired twice in reaction though this did not accomplish a thing.

Harry, still keeping the wall as a barrier, fired again as the assassin attempted with painful effort to roll out of the way. Luck had not altogether deserted the man, though it was just about to. The .44 sped into the bed, its impact muffled by the mattress stuffing in which it was eventually ensnared.

Despite the enormity of the pain and the certainty of his impending death, for to live would mean enduring life as a cripple from the waist down, the assassin blindly turned his 9mm Short away from Harry, directing it under the bed, hoping to hit Owens and in that way take somebody else with him when he went out.

He managed to get off two more rounds before Harry's bullet slammed into his chest, plowing through his right lung and out his back, thereby quickening his end. He flopped back, one hand clasped hold of the entry wound, feebly pushing against it as if to stem the tide of blood. Desperately, he made an effort to raise his head but could not. A wind-like sound whistled through him, and as it emerged from his lips he died.

Now Harry drew himself fully erect and entered the bedroom.

"Drake?" he called out, "Drake, are you all right?"

When he received no reply, he grew alarmed and got down on his knees to better look underneath the bed.

Owens was lying there, but he was unmoving. Harry maneuvered the bed out of the way so he could get closer to him.

Blood was seeping out of two wounds that had entered his side, one appeared to have gone into his abdomen, the other into his chest. He was still alive but barely conscious. His eyes followed Harry, but he seemed unable to talk.

"You'll be all right, goddamn you, you're going to make it," Harry kept saying over and over. It was the nearest he ever got to praying.

With sheets he tore from the bed and ripped into smaller pieces, he tightly bound the two wounds to staunch the bleeding. But there wasn't much blood to be staunched. Far greater was the danger from the internal injuries, and there was no way Harry could determine just how grave these were.

He reached for the phone, fearing that the assassin might have cut the line, but the phone was still in service.

With the terseness of a veteran detective he explained his situation to the police, emphasizing the need for an ambulance and medical assistance.

Perhaps because of his impatience, the police seemed to take an unusually long time in getting to the Ninn residence. In the interval Harry had managed to throw on a shirt and trousers and to discover, as he had expected, that Ninn had been murdered. The television was still going, but the station that was on was broadcasting "The Star Spangled Banner" before signing off.

Harry neglected to turn the TV off though, and even as the ambulance screamed up the street and police officers invaded the house, with guns drawn as though they anticipated a firefight that had gone on and ended without them, the test pattern remained, buzzing like a deranged horde of mosquitoes about to attack.

Chapter Fourteen

"I understand that your friend is to be operated on again today," the solemn-faced man with hair the color of the Antarctic was saying. This was Detective Sergeant Matt Butterfield of the LAPD, and he sat behind his desk with his hands folded rather in the manner of an obedient schoolboy.

Harry was sitting across from him, his face expressive of an exhaustion that is so total it is no longer worth trying to do anything about.

"That's right. They performed emergency surgery last night. But there's still another bullet lodged in him. They're hoping to extract it today." He looked to his watch. "They should be in surgery right now."

"What do the doctors say?"

Harry shrugged. "They're hopeful. Cautiously optimistic, as they say. But they don't know if he'll pull out of it. It's too early to tell."

Butterfield nodded. He then unfolded his hands and thrust forward a collection of photographs, most of them taken in a precinct house. They were all of the same man, who wore a look of detachment so pronounced he could have been posing for his wedding picture rather than for a booking on attempted murder charges.

Harry had no trouble identifying the man in these photographs. He was the man he had killed the night before.

"His name's Tom Loving. Otherwise known as 'Pigeon.' "

"Pigeon?"

"People thought he resembled one. A rat with wings, you know? Turns out he also raised pigeons, racing them for a while. Weird fellow, could never keep him locked up for longer than a couple of years. Best we could stick him with was assault and battery or attempted armed robbery, shit like that. Always managed to beat the system, got out the last time because the probation board noted his good behavior." Butterfield released a bitter laugh. "Good behavior, that fucker probably didn't know the meaning of good behavior when he was at his mother's tit."

"Mafia?"

"No, free-lance. A good reliable asshole like him, he gets calls from all over the state. Last I heard he was operating in San Diego, which was why I was surprised he turned up here."

"He known for arson?"

"Arson?" Butterfield shrugged. "He's never been charged with that particular crime, but I certainly wouldn't put it past him. He's very innovative in the way he carries out his hits. Try anything once, see if it works." He indicated the chonta that overnight had been transformed from a murder weapon to state's evidence. "Imported from South America. Very effective. Our pathologist tells us that Mr. Ninn must have been dead within seconds."

Harry nodded unhappily.

"You think that he could have been responsible for the slayings we've had in San Francisco?" Harry asked, observing the weapon. It was his sense that the hit man could not have been, but he wanted to see what Butterfield had to say.

Butterfield agreed with him. "From what I've read and heard about those beheadings, I'd have to say no. They sound to me like a man gone off the deep end. Pathological, you know? And Pigeon was pathological all right, but he wouldn't go about killing people in the same way. Not with so much blood. With him everything was, well, I guess the word for it is discreet."

He now thrust forward a slip of paper so that Harry could inspect it. All it said was "X801."

"We found it on Pigeon when we did a thorough search of his body. You have any idea what it might mean?"

Harry shook his head.

"I thought it might be a license plate or something like that. We're checking it out with the Registry of Motor Vehicles here and in San Francisco, but I'm not really hopeful anything'll come of it."

As Harry was rising to leave, for all the necessary information had been exchanged between the two men, Butterfield urged him to stay in touch. "I have a feeling we're going to see a development in this case real soon."

"I wish I could say the same."

Harry drove immediately to the hospital where Owens was being cared for. The case had become secondary in his mind because of his concern for his partner. All he could think of was that the miserable luck that had stalked all his previous partners still persisted, like some demon that he could not, whatever prayers and potions he tried, be exorcised.

Last night, in his confrontation with Pigeon, he had been afraid. There was always fear there, there was no way to escape it, and in most instances he found the fear was a healthy thing, like pain. Better than indifference, better by far than numbness. But that fear had been nothing compared to the dread he felt hours later when he had had to telephone Mary Beth and tell her what had happened to her husband.

Because he felt both responsible and guilty, because he kept going back over the shooting in his mind, wondering whether he could have done something sooner, or differently, to prevent harm from coming to Owens, he was prepared for an angry, reproachful response from Mary Beth.

She had been sleeping when he'd called but came instantly awake. And far from being in any way accusatory, she accepted the news as calmly as she could, telling him that she would be on the next available shuttle flight to Los Angeles.

Harry found her in the waiting room that adjoined the emergency area. It was getting on toward noon, and the area was alive with activity. There were a great many more people seeking emergency aid than usual because of the fires, and for hours, as Mary Beth waited for her husband to come out of surgery, men and women, bruised and battered and burned, paraded before her, some of them silent, their lips pursed in defiance of their pain, others crying out in protest and agony. The atmosphere was far from soothing, and in Harry's eyes it could only heighten her tension and fear.

He greeted her and sat down beside her. Though her eyes were red, she was no longer crying, and she seemed composed though abstracted.

"There's a coffee shop in this hospital, it might be better to wait there. I'll come with you if you want."

"No, I want to be here when the operation's over. I want to be here."

She asked him in detail how Owens had sustained his injuries, and Harry gave her as accurate an account as he could, omitting some of the more sordid particulars.

"Poor Mac," she kept saying. "Poor Mac. You say he died instantly? I suppose then that it was better than suffering." Her knuckles were white, and to stop her hands from trembling she knitted them together in her lap.

After sitting together like this for a few minutes in an uncomfortable silence, Harry decided that he would have to leave. He promised he would call in an hour, when the procedure was expected to end, and stood there for a moment, uncertain as to whether there was anything else to say, any assurance or consolation he could give. He realized there was nothing.

Mary Beth raised her eyes to him. "Thank you, Harry. For all you've done, thank you. And don't blame yourself for what's happened. That would be terrible."

It was like a priest absolving him of sin. But the truth was that even Mary Beth, even Owens if he recovered, could not do that. Only he himself could, and he didn't know if that was possible.

He now went back to Ocean Boulevard. Where the house belonging to Eloise Cummings and Patience Bell had stood there was only a smoldering ruin. The remaining walls had gone from white to black; the bedroom on the second floor, charred and still wet from all the water that had been used to douse the flames, was exposed to view. Harry could see the closets, now just more rubble and ash, where the two extravagant ladies had stocked their lavish collection of clothing.

As he stood there, staring at the house, he noticed another woman who was standing on the adjacent lawn. She was probably close to thirty, with brown hair that was let loose down her back and wearing a long blue dress. She looked as if she hadn't quite gotten over the Sixties. She had the style and manner of a veteran of Haight-Ashbury who was aging gracefully but aging all the same.

"Do you live next door?" Harry asked.

She nodded, hastening to add so Harry would not get any ideas, "With my husband."

Harry strode toward her. "Quite a fire last night," he said, keeping his voice neutral. "I happened to see it."

"It almost got out of control. For a while there I thought we might lose our house, too. We had all our things packed and were ready to evacuate. Thank God, that wasn't necessary."

The woman introduced herself as Alice David. Harry mentioned that he was a police officer and showed her his identification. Either she did not see or did not care that he represented the San Francisco force.

"You investigating the fire? There were men here all this morning, sifting through the rubble. They say it was arson that did it."

"Not exactly the fire. More like the house itself. And the women who occupied it. Did you know them?"

"You mean Patience and Eloise? I used to see them if that's what you mean. I don't think anyone really knew them except for the men that'd keep marching in and out of the house. They didn't have other girlfriends. And most of the men friends weren't exactly friends, if you catch my meaning."

Harry caught it all right.

"Would you say that they made their living from prostitution?"

"I don't think you'd be jumping to any conclusion. That would be my guess. They must have paid a mint for their clothes."

"They did indeed."

"Mmmmm," she said as though a hunch had just been confirmed. "I think though that basically they weren't straight at all. I have a feeling they were lezies. Gay, you know?" You'd never see one without the other. They were inseparable, and they were both good-looking, more than good-looking actually, and probably they had a package deal going for the men. Two for the price of one, you know? But I'd say they were contemptuous of the men, of all men."

"Ever see a repeat, I mean one man in particular who kept coming back?"

"Let's see." Alice turned thoughtful for a few moments. "Yes, there was one. Middle-aged. Handsome if you like them like that."

"Like what?"

"Oh, big-boned, businessman type. Austere. Probably a jock in college. Gray-haired, carefully cut and styled. He stood out because he looked so wealthy, so much in command of the situation. What I remember most was that once he came he used to stay as long as he liked. Sometimes through the night, at least for several hours, usually during the afternoons. And that was a privilege none of the other men ever got. I suppose he was just paying so much more, and it was undoubtedly easier on the girls, handling one guy instead of a dozen."

"How many times would this man visit?"

"Five, six times a month maybe. But then the girls would go away for a while, it wasn't as though they were there continuously. I wonder what they'll think when they find out this has happened." She looked over at the hulk their home had become.

"I don't think they're going to worry about it much," Harry remarked without elaboration. "Did you ever know what this man's name was?"

"Well, as I said, I never said more than good-morning or good-night to them, but I once heard them going on about somebody they referred to as Teddy. Teddy this and Teddy that, and do we really want to go up to San Francisco again, such a drag. They'd lay out nude in their backyard and they'd gossip like mad out there, and when they started an argument, you know, with Patience wanting to go up to San Francisco, and Eloise saying no, you could hear them all over the neighborhood."

"Any family, any relatives you know of?"

"I'm sure they cut them all off years ago. Or vice versa, more likely. They lived in that place for four or five years, before we moved into this neighborhood, and to them, you know, Christmas was like any other day. Fuck a few more men, put more money in the bank." She sounded oddly resentful. She was undoubtedly happy to see such destruction visited upon them. She didn't know the half of it.

"Tell me, Mrs. David, what kind of transportation did this middle-aged man, Teddy, employ to get here?"

"It varied. I'd see him roll up in a white Porsche, but once or twice he arrived in a limo. One of those block-long gas-guzzlers with the sunroof? He used to have his chauffeur wait for hours for him. Driver would just sit there and read. I felt so sorry for him one time I brought him out some coffee."

Harry had stopped listening. Something the woman had said about the limousine had sparked a sudden inspiration. The cryptic set of digits preceded by an equally cryptic X returned to his memory. "Mrs. David, do you mind if I use your phone for a moment? It's long distance to San Francisco, but I will compensate you for it. But it's urgent that I call."

She seemed surprised by the intensity in his voice but had no objection to his using the phone.

It was perhaps little more than a wild guess, but it was just possible that he had something, that he had figured out the meaning of X801.

There was a slight delay as the transmission was completed. Then he heard the predictably upbeat voice on the other end: "Good morning. Cavanaugh-Sterling International."

Harry paused for a moment, then requested the office he had called only a few days before. "Extension 801," he said.

Another brief wait. Then a young woman's voice: "Mr. Davis' office, can I help you?"

Little did the secretary know it, but she already had. Harry hung up, reasonably certain that he now knew who had hired Tom "Pigeon" Loving. And further, he also felt that he knew who exactly Teddy was. "That son of a bitch," he said aloud.

Alice scowled at him. "What?"

He turned around. He had forgotten she was right there beside him.

"I need to make just one more call, Mrs. David."

"Go ahead. Can I get you some coffee? A Coke?"

"Nothing, thanks."

He now dialed the hospital. As he waited for the doctor to respond to the page, he grew increasingly apprehensive. On the one hand, he felt exhilarated at finally uncovering the Tocador killer. On the other, he recognized that bad news about Owens would dampen that exhilaration and cause his triumph to pall.

At last the doctor—a polite but somewhat authoritarian figure who did not like to disclose more facts than he had to and who remained extremely cautious when it came to predicting the outcome of his cases—came on the line. "Ah, how are you, Mr. Callahan? What can I do for you?"

As if he didn't know. Harry reminded himself not to loose his temper at this man—wouldn't do any good.

"I would like to know how the surgery on my partner Drake Owens went."

"Generally speaking, it went as well as could be expected under the circumstances."

"What does that mean?"

"It means that we have successfully removed the bullet. He has lost a considerable amount of blood, and we had to give him an additional three pints. He is now in recovery, and shortly we will send him up to the intensive care unit."

"What are his chances, Doctor?"

"I would say that they are fifty-fifty, marginally better than they were last night."

"I would like to see him."

"I am afraid that no visitors are allowed at present. If he is coming along by tomorrow perhaps then. . . ."

But Harry did not have time to wait in Los Angeles until tomorrow. He reached Mary Beth at the Holiday Inn on Wilshire, where she had gone after Owens had emerged from surgery, and told her that he was returning to San Francisco. "If anything happens let me know immediately," he urged her, "and I'll be back as quickly as I can."

"I think it'll be all right, Harry. The doctor tells me he's almost out of the woods." She did not sound nearly as optimistic as one would have inferred from the words alone. "And I hope that I don't have to disturb you."

"That's the last thing you should be worrying about," Harry said before hanging up.

And now he had to face another challenge: proving absolutely that William Davis, chairman of the board of Cavanaugh-Sterling, and the demented murderer Teddy were one and the same, and then putting him away before he could do any further harm. Neither task was going to be easy.

Chapter Fifteen

As Harry was walking toward his office, on the seventh floor of the Justice Building, he was stopped by Bressler, who happened to be coming in the other direction.

"Well?" he said. "What have you got?"

"Pieces," Harry tersely replied. "I'm trying to put them together."

"How's Owens coming along?"

"When I talked to the doctor before I left L.A. he had a fifty-fifty chance."

"That's more than a lot of people get." Bressler used cynicism to conceal the very real pain that he, like any other cop, felt when death threatened one of their own. "How soon are you going to have those pieces put together?"

"Very soon."

"It better be. I am tired of taking flak in this case. I am tired of losing officers, I am tired of losing credibility. You better deliver something good."

"If I deliver it'll be good."

"I wish I could believe that." Bressler began to walk away, then he stopped suddenly and said, "By the way, that fellow Davis get ahold of you?"

"Davis? You mean William Davis?"

"That's right. He said he had some information for you,

wouldn't say what it was, said he needed to speak to you immediately. I told him that you were flying down to L.A. and gave him the address where you and Drake were staying. Did he reach you all right?"

Now Harry understood how Teddy's man Pigeon had managed to track them down.

"Oh yes," Harry answered, "he certainly reached me all right."

Bressler shot him a curious look, sensing that Harry was holding back an important detail, but when Harry failed to elaborate, he merely shrugged and continued on his way.

Harry decided to turn right around, forget about checking on the messages and paperwork that had piled up on his desk during his brief absence. He resolved instead to go to Davis' home—one of his three homes, the one inhabited by Davis' wife.

He realized that Davis would not be there and in fact hoped that he would not be. If Davis was the man he sought, and after what Bressler had just disclosed, he had even more reason to believe he was, then he could not take him directly, not yet. He intended to circle around him, close in on him, maybe force his hand.

His wife, he hoped, would be the place to begin.

Sheila Davis lived in a large, but hardly overwhelming, villa that overlooked Tiburon's waterfront with its cluster of restaurants, galleries, antique shops and marinas that lined Main Street. Like the neighboring villas set into the hillside, it was painted a pastel hue, in this case, lemon. In its architecture and situation, it brought to mind an aristocrat's home on the Mediterranean.

A woman came to the door and squinted at Harry. She was obviously the maid, a Chicano slightly stooped by the years and by her labor. She had difficulty comprehending what Harry was saying.

"Who is it, Maria?" Harry heard a woman call out.

Then Sheila Davis herself came to the door. She looked much like she had in the photograph Davis kept on his desk: pale and vulnerable, tentative about her movements as though nothing was to be depended on, even the sustaining pull of gravity.

Harry displayed his I.D. for her.

"Oh?" she said. "You've come about that terrorist attack. I've talked to your people before. I don't know whether I can add anything but please come on in."

Harry said nothing to disabuse her of her assumption. He did not want to say anything just yet that might suggest he was more interested in putting her husband behind bars than he was in putting away the men who'd tried to kill him.

She escorted him into a den that was lined on two walls with bookshelves. The books were all impressively bound in leather, but what astonished Harry, when he observed how they were arranged, was that all the books were of the same width. The Bible and *War and Peace* and Dickens' *A Tale of Two Cities* matched exactly as did several hundred others.

Sheila had left him alone for a minute while she went to prepare some coffee for them both, so Harry was allowed the freedom to investigate this small but tantalizing mystery. He reached out and grabbed one of the books. Opening it, he discovered that the pages were blank, that in fact the insides of the whole collection, at least in this room, were blank. Only an impressive cover and empty inside. Just like their owner.

There were also photographs on the walls, most of them framed and protected under glass. One showed Davis standing on the prow of a boat holding up a swordfish that he had just snared. He was grinning in triumph, gesturing to whomever had taken the picture. At the bottom, on the right side, Harry found a notation: "To Teddy—The Master of Dumb Luck." It was signed "Chuck."

At that moment Sheila entered the room, bearing a tray with two cups and a silver coffeepot.

"Tell me, Mrs. Davis, why is your husband referred to here as Teddy?"

She laughed. "Chuck, his best friend Chuck, calls him that. It's a kind of nickname I'd guess you'd say. They go way back to when they were in high school together, which is why Bill lets him get away with it. If I called him Teddy, he'd go wild. Actually, almost nobody outside a small circle of friends knows he has a nickname."

"How did he get it?"

Harry tried to make the question sound as offhand as possible.

"I think the story is that he was rather chubby in high school, and somebody thought he resembled a teddy bear." She regarded Harry curiously, wondering perhaps why he was so interested in such a trivial matter.

"Just one more thing, Mrs. Davis. Has your husband shown any sign of tension, emotional distress that might have followed from the attack made on his life?" Harry was striving to make his question sound innocent, even sympathetic.

Sheila frowned. "My husband is a very closed-in man, and in all our twenty-two years of marriage I have seldom seen him display any emotional distress. He may get angry, but he doesn't really express that anger. You can almost see him fighting it back. But to tell you the truth, in the last several months I so rarely see him that I can't really give you an accurate idea. It may be that he releases all those pent-up emotions with somebody else. Not with me. I am a victim, as they say, of benign neglect."

When Harry left Sheila Davis and returned by ferry to San Francisco, he contemplated his dilemma. He was convinced that Davis was his man, but he had grave doubts that he could lock him up with what he had. There was only circumstantial evidence—the coincidence of names, the possible identification of Davis by the woman who lived next door to Patience and Eloise—but nothing hard that could firmly tie Davis in with the slayings at the Tocador and the twenty-four-hour sex club on Folsom. Yet to delay further, while he scavenged about for the "smoking gun" that might constitute absolute proof, would allow Teddy to remain at large, with the freedom to commit another act of mayhem.

Harry saw now that to wait any longer might be a worse idea than risking an immediate arrest. Though placing Davis under constant surveillance was a possibility, he doubted very much whether it would be effective. Davis was too shrewd, too protected, and he would soon be alerted to the surveillance and take steps to avoid it.

He dialed Cavanaugh-Sterling's Headquarters and again asked for extension 801.

"Mr. Davis is not here right now," his secretary said, "but I know that he's anxious to speak with you, Inspector."

Harry asked if he could see him as soon as he got back to his office.

"Why don't you come by around eight-thirty? Mr. Davis will be working late tonight."

"Eight-thirty it is."

"Fine. I am certain Mr. Davis is looking forward to seeing you again."

"I wouldn't doubt it."

"Have a good day," she perfunctorily wished him, neglecting to note the fact that the day was over.

The man standing across the street from Cavanaugh-Sterling Headquarters recognized Harry when he started up the stairs to the entrance. He recalled him from a day back in mid-October when this man had pursued him across the rooftops of the very buildings in whose shadows he now maintained his vigil.

The sight of this man, whom he knew to be a police officer,

unsettled him. Was it possible, he wondered, that Davis realized he would be attacked again tonight and had called upon this man to help him?

Nonetheless, he would not recommend cancelling the assault. It had been too long in planning, too much depended on it. And in any case, if Davis truly did suspect trouble, wouldn't he have sent for several policemen and not just one solitary officer? This thought reassured the man. He returned to his men and told them that everything was as it should be; the operation could go ahead as scheduled.

Chapter Sixteen

The night staff on duty at Cavanaugh-Sterling Headquarters was considerably smaller than the daytime one. Not unexpectedly, there were the ever present security guards loitering about. Otherwise, there were only the custodians sadly pursuing their nocturnal duties and the cleaning ladies lugging vacuum cleaners and pails filled with soapy water from empty office to empty office.

Harry presented himself at the front desk in the lobby and, after being cleared, was given a plastic-sealed card that confirmed his status as official visitor. He signed his name and time in the log book, then proceeded to the elevator bank.

It was eerily quiet along the fortieth-floor corridor. Even the cleaning ladies had gone. Nonetheless, Harry had the sense that he was being watched, and not just by the video cameras that peeked out from various corners of the hallway, but by human beings whose job it was to protect the chairman of the board of Cavanaugh-Sterling from harm.

But Davis was alone in his office from all appearances. His secretary had gone, and the waiting room was empty. The door to his office was closed, but Harry could hear a rustling of papers and the squeak of the swivel chair that signaled Davis' presence within.

It would not have surprised Harry to learn that Davis was

watching him on a closed-circuit TV system, for though he hadn't announced himself Davis was already calling to him. "Mr. Callahan, please come in."

Harry opened the door and stepped into the office. There, as he'd expected, sitting behind his desk was Davis, looking as fit and as authoritative as ever. He was working in his shirtsleeves, his jacket draped over the back of his chair. For several moments he continued writing on the papers he had in front of him, what seemed to be some kind of contracts, signing his name with a flourish. He purposely ignored Harry who approached the desk.

"Sit down, please, I'll be with you in just a minute."

When Harry did so, Davis at last directed his eyes toward him and gave him a smile that was as gracious as it was convincing.

At that very instant there was a low hum from each side of the office, and as Harry turned first to the left and then to the right he saw that it had been caused by the paneled walls opening up. As there were secret corridors and exits and entrances in the tortured soul of William Maxim Davis so were there secret corridors and exits and entrances in the offices and homes that he inhabited.

Emerging from each side of the office, stepping out of small adjoining rooms that looked as dark and claustrophobic as monks' cloisters, were two security men, in plainclothes but very clearly armed. They carried in their hands converted Smith and Wesson Model 39s, the principal difference between the converted and original being improved accuracy and a reduction in length, height, width, and weight for maximum concealment. They contained a clip of eight rounds each which would mean that before Harry could get out his own weapon and do much of anything with it, he would very likely find his body riddled with sixteen rounds.

This prospect did not strike him as a very pleasing one, and, even as he cursed himself for blundering into Davis' trap he tossed aside his .44, complying with the order Davis had just given him, almost casually, for he was still working on his contracts, signing his name over and over again as though he wanted to prove just how meaningless he had ever viewed the threat that Harry had posed.

Harry remained seated, saying nothing—what was there to say with two guns targeted at your head?—waiting for Davis to conclude his business and get to the point which, he supposed glumly, was his imminent execution.

Eventually, Davis put his final signature on paper and rose from his desk. As he slipped on his jacket, he said, "Now, I trust you will prove cooperative, Mr. Callahan. It would serve no one's interests if you attempted to resist us. I would not want to have you killed here. It would be an embarrassment for us, but it would be something much more grievous for you. So if you'll come along quietly, and bear in mind that my men will keep their eyes and their weapons fixed on you at all times, I would be most appreciative."

The rigid etiquette he stuck to even in such circumstances seemed totally incongruous to Harry, but he was in no position to point this out.

Davis himself appropriated the .44. "A curious instrument," he remarked turning it over in his hand. "And very effective, too, I'd imagine."

"Very," Harry agreed.

They walked down the corridor to the elevators, four solemn uncommunicative men, and they descended in the same way: without a word or so much as an exchange of glances.

As they proceeded by the security desk in the lobby, Davis turned to Harry and with forced jocularity said, "Don't forget to give back your visitor's pass and sign out in the log."

This is all getting to be a bit much, Harry thought, but he did as he was instructed.

They began down the marble steps that led from the Cavanaugh-Sterling complex. Harry was flanked on both sides by the security men and Davis was right in back of him.

There seemed to be no way that he could escape or overcome his antagonists quickly enough to avoid being fatally shot.

A big black limousine pulled up in front of them. A chauffeur promptly got out of it and threw open the rear door.

"No white Porsche tonight?" asked Harry, feeling free to say whatever he wanted since it appeared that his fate had already been decided.

Davis did not take exception to the comment. He seemed actually to enjoy the jibe. "Regrettably, I was compelled to discard the Porsche."

As they neared the limo, Harry asked where they were going.

Davis' response was characteristically cryptic but telling: "Someplace quiet."

Davis signaled to the chauffeur that his presence was no longer required. "You can go home now. I will drive."

This switch apparently surprised both the security guards for their otherwise implacable expressions subtly altered.

"I used to be quite the driver, Mr. Callahan. I drove in the Grand Prix, did you know that?"

"Did you win?"

"Came in fourth. I gave it up after that. I do not like engaging in competitions that I can't win."

Davis gestured for Harry to slide over to the other side of the front seat. The two bodyguards slid into the rear. That Davis failed to open up what Harry presumed to be the bulletproof partition separating front from back astonished him somewhat. It could not have been forgetfulness on Davis' part. He wasn't a man to forget the slightest detail. Obviously, he had enough confidence in his control over the situation that the men in back were only of secondary importance to him.

As Davis began to maneuver the limo away from the curb, Ha[illegible] asked him what he had against the women he'd butche[illegible] What crime did Martha Denby commit? Or

Patience Bell and Eloise Cummings? Besides screwing around a lot, which I'm not sure is a crime, let alone one punishable by death?"

Davis glanced back, a bit nervously, but the two men comfortably installed in the rear gave no sign that they had heard the question. The partition was resistant to sound as well as to bullets. That explained one reason why Davis had left the partition in place, Harry realized.

He kept his eyes on the darkened street ahead of him. "They all wanted to be in pictures, Mr. Callahan, did you know that? Only Martha showed any talent for it. Eloise and Patience, I think, had been on every casting couch in L.A. before I met them. But they had a certain élan that I liked, a spirit." He was going on in the manner of an actor giving a monologue. There was no indication that he had heard Harry's question correctly or if he had, he certainly didn't intend to answer it head-on. Maybe because he couldn't.

"Oh yes, I suppose it was the idea that I would be getting two of them. They were like twins, so responsive to each other's thoughts and movements that if I got one to come the other would come just watching the two of us. Or sometimes she didn't have to be in the same room, as astonishing as it may seem to you. Sometimes she could be elsewhere in the house, vacuuming the rug, reading a book, and it wouldn't matter, she'd sustain an orgasm, too."

A curious use of the word "sustain," Harry thought, recognizing simultaneously that this man was more unhinged than he had originally hypothesized.

"But then, you know," Davis continued, his voice growing more disembodied, more hollow and emotionless, "you tire of things. The girls were violating their accord to me. They were not to engage in sex with any other men. But they ignored me. It was as though they were sending a message to me: Teddy, you're not good enough to satisfy us, you're just not good enough. And as I just told you, I am not interested in competitions where I cannot emerge the winner."

"So you invited them up to San Francisco and killed them?"

"Exactly. I chose an out-of-the-way hotel simply because it was just that, out of the way, an unlikely place for a killing."

"And Miss Denby?"

"I held Martha in great esteem, although I doubt whether you would believe me. I was going to take her to Acapulco when the movie was over. I bought Global because it would give me access to women like Martha and Eloise. And Patience. Did you know that? But like the others, Martha defied me. I tested her, I wanted to see how she would react to temptation. And she fell."

When you listened to him it all seemed so eerily simple. No tangled emotions, no passion, no stirrings of conscience, certainly no remorse. It was a job, one two three, over and done with.

At the intersection of Alvarado and Castro, a green and white Mercury shot out in front of them and stopped, so surprising Davis that it was all he could do to slam on the brakes and bring his car to a halt just before it smashed into the Mercury.

"The hell?" He looked to Harry as though he expected him to have an explanation.

Another car, a Pontiac, came up from behind them and smashed the limousine in the rear, giving a terrific jolt to its occupants, stunning the two guards as their heads collided with the partition.

Yet a third vehicle, a VW van pulled up alongside of them, effectively cornering the limo in.

It was apparent to them all what has happening even before the van's doors slid open, revealing three men brandishing Belgian FN MAG machine guns, the same type that had been employed in the attempt on Davis the last time.

Now the Mercury disgorged its passengers: another group of three, also armed with automatics. They crept behind their car and used it as protection.

The trio in the VW opened up, their bullets spraying the windows along their right side without, however, penetrating. It sounded like a very severe hailstorm.

Davis, taking confidence from their failure, decided to crash his way out of his predicament. With his foot pressed firmly down on the gas, he propelled the limousine forward in the direction of the Mercury.

A salvo of gunfire caused the windshield to splinter and crack in so many places that visibility decreased nearly to zero. But Davis didn't need to see to find the Mercury. His face lit up, excitement burned in his eyes. Harry, looking at him, thought that this must be what he was like when he was racing cars in the Grand Prix. This was what he must be like when he decapitated his victims.

In back, the two bodyguards sat nervously, one wiping blood off his forehead. Though they both had their guns in their hands, there wasn't very much they could do with them unless they chose to open the windows, which would be tantamount to committing suicide.

Harry braced himself for the collision, holding his hands against the edge of the dashboard.

The impact was accompanied by an incredible din of metal and glass twisting and clattering apart. The Mercury buckled and reeled back, like a wounded bull, but then it came bouncing to a stop, its chassis upside down, its wheels churning futilely in the air. Two of the terrorists lay crushed and bleeding beneath it. A third had somehow caught onto one of the wheels and lay, dying on top, his entrails oozing slowly out of a great tear in his gut.

The limousine itself had gone as far as it was ever going to get, halted finally by the overturned Mercury, its front welded into the obliterated wreckage of the other car.

From the back, intense fire from both the VW and the Pontiac continued. But the lead-based windows of the limousine withstood even this latest fusillade.

Davis had been flung up against the steering wheel and while not seriously harmed, was momentarily disabled.

Harry didn't wait. He grabbed hold of Davis and flung him to the right, meeting no resistance. At the same time he slid his hand into his jacket pocket and withdrew his .44.

Simultaneously, the partition slid open. The security men in back, still operative despite the collision, held up their guns, training them on Harry. What Harry had not realized was that an emergency control existed in back to work the partition. But it made sense now that he thought about it; the back was where Davis usually sat.

It was a Mexican stand-off in the true meaning of the phrase, for while the limousine could move no farther the terrorists could not take advantage of its immobility as long as the car remained sealed. And while the two security men could easily kill Harry, they did not dare to fire as long as Harry had his .44 aimed at their employer who now regarded Harry with a dazed, almost sorrowful expression. It did not seem that he truly comprehended what was happening.

"It'll do you no good," Davis mumbled to Harry, meaning, Harry presumed, that killing him would not achieve the end he'd hoped for.

Harry noticed that he kept stealing glances at the steering wheel or rather, just slightly below it, where the emergency brake was located.

Without removing his eyes from Davis, he surreptitiously moved his free hand forward, while at the same time concealing this movement from view by shifting his body slightly.

The terrorists had redoubled their efforts, it seemed, for the rattle of gunfire was growing ever louder, and the cacophony was nearly deafening, what with all the hundreds of rounds striking, then rebounding off the windows and pinging crazily against the battered chassis.

All that Harry's hand touched was a small toggle switch

under the dashboard. There was nothing else. He had no idea what it would do, what importance it held, and whether in fact that this was what seemed to worry Davis.

"It shouldn't have to end this way," Davis was saying. "It was supposed to end, of course, things could not keep on going like this, but this was not the end that I had planned." He seemed oblivious to the terrorist attack that was going on around him, and oblivious, too, to the men whom he had taken along to protect him.

"What do you want us to do?" the one on his right asked. "What do you want us to do?"

Perhaps he hoped that Davis would sign his own death warrant by consenting to Harry's execution. For there was no way that the guards could take out Harry without ensuring that Davis would receive a .44 round between his eyes first.

But Davis didn't seem to hear what the man had said, for he continued to ignore him. His eyes narrowed as though he was struggling to articulate a very difficult and confusing thought. Either the collision had shocked him more than Harry had surmised or he was just headed farther off the deep end, but in any case he was no longer aware of anything other than Harry.

Harry still had his hand—actually just his two middle fingers—on the toggle switch. The only thought that came into his mind was this: What the hell, why not? The situation can't get any worse than it already is. Somebody's got to die.

And with that he pulled the switch.

For a second nothing at all happened, and Harry concluded that maybe the switch was an innocuous thing that controlled an emergency light or some such thing.

But then there was a muffled roar and a flash of light and a cascade of blood that came down on them as though the roof of the car had suddenly begun to let loose a rainstorm. Three shotgun shells had just been jettisoned in rapid succession into Davis' ass and torn him into hundreds of pieces inside and out, allowing him not even the time for a scream, let alone a last-minute prayer.

Harry was rocked back in his seat by the force of the blast, and his ears rang from the concussive sound it produced. And for several additional moments it was nearly impossible for him to see. His eyes were covered with blood and viscera, and his whole body was strewn with bits and pieces of William Maxim Davis, who was now all over the interior of the car.

But he reacted swiftly enough even so, wiping the blood from his eyes. Still holding on tight to the .44, he fired over the back of his seat, hitting one of the guards in the head. The bullet entered the man's ear and took away practically half of his skull as it exited.

His companion, too, had been temporarily overcome by the explosion that had taken Davis' life and he did not recover in time to pose serious opposition to Harry. He fired, but because his vision was still obscured, his bullet struck only the windshield.

Harry, in turn, discharged his .44. The guard lurched forward, then tipped backward, coming to a rest at last atop the container reserved for the Piper Heidseick champagne.

The terrorists had in the meantime moved up around the limousine, perhaps attracted by the sight of so much blood erupting inside of it. Or maybe they feared the imminent arrival of the police and had resolved on taking decisive action now.

Harry didn't care to determine what their motivation was. He opened the door and threw himself out on the ground.

Two of the terrorists were approaching from the left side, and when Harry dropped right in front of them, they didn't immediately shoot. Being so spattered with blood, Harry looked as though he was dead enough already.

Their momentary hesitation proved fatal. From his prone position, Harry shot one and then the other, hitting the first in the chest, the second in the legs. The former staggered back, and then with his arms outstretched crucifix-fashion, he crumpled to the ground. The second toppled over in pain, howling in anguish, simultaneously releasing hold of his FN.

Harry raced forward, shooting again. The terrorist who'd been struggling to get back upright gave up. Harry retrieved the FN and loosened a barrage from it just as a third assailant appeared, wondering what had happened.

The rounds from the FN took him apart from his sternum to nearly his crotch, like a zipper opening up to reveal an ever widening stream of blood. Like an undulating dancer, he dropped back, then down.

From several blocks away sirens shrieked, and that was cue enough for the surviving terrorists to retreat. After directing some desultory fire at Harry, they sought refuge in the VW van. The bearded man who took the wheel began to reverse the van back down Castro, toward Market, because with access to Alavadro blocked completely by the combined wreckage of the Lincoln and the Mercury, no other choice was available.

Harry rushed out and faced the escaping VW. Crouching, he directed the FN at the windshield of the van. Unlike the limousine, the VW did not have the protection of bulletproof glass. The glass shattered, and the driver dropped out of sight, presumably incapacitated if not killed. Another man sought to take control of the wheel before the vehicle skidded into the abandoned Pontiac. This second driver knew enough to keep his head down, so Harry contented himself with shooting out the forward tires.

The van began to respond to the injuries it was taking and wove back and forth along the street, its front chassis sagging as the rubber tires came apart.

Then, whether because the front wheels had given out or because the driver couldn't adequately control the van, the VW veered sharply to the left and lifted up onto the sidewalk, crashing against the cement steps of an apartment building.

The only way for the van to get back onto the street again was to go forward, but by doing this, the driver brought the van directly into Harry's line of fire.

Evidently, the three surviving terrorists decided to abandon the VW, seeing as how it had outlasted its usefulness.

To avoid being cut down all at once, they wisely chose to leave each by a different way—one out each of the front doors, the last out of the sliding door in back.

Harry could bring down only the two men who emerged from the right side, catching one in mid-leap and the other only an instant after he'd hit the ground.

But the man who'd been doing the driving managed to elude him and began running down Castro, zigzagging in expectation of the rounds that Harry would send after him.

However, there were now two police cruisers, side by side, speeding up Castro in his direction. Seeing that he was trapped, the terrorist turned to confront Harry.

For a brief instant the two looked at one another. Harry remembered the terrorist just as the terrorist remembered Harry.

It was like a duel in a Western, the two men facing each other off, both with guns raised in their hands, knowing that one or the other, maybe both, will have to die.

The terrorist opened up just as Harry threw himself to the ground. A hail of bullets sailed in the air over his body and so close that he could feel the heat of them as they passed.

When he'd hit the ground, Harry had lost hold of the FN. He had no alternative but to rely on the .44, which he fired as accurately as possible—because this was the final round he had in the clip, and he'd never have time to reload.

The bullet caught the terrorist high up on his chest, in the niche formed at the division of the collarbone. Blood gurgled from the wound. The terrorist discarded his automatic to clutch the injury with both hands. He did not fall at once but instead staggered madly in circles. Finally, the effort did not seem worth it to him any longer, and he sank to the ground.

Harry approached him and watched him die.

Four police officers, their guns drawn, cautiously moved up the street in their direction.

The terrorist gazed up at Harry, with an expression almost prayerful in its intensity. When he opened his mouth to speak, blood began to drain out. Harry stooped close to him to better hear his final words.

"I hated Davis," he mumbled, "I hated that man."

"You and me both," said Harry.

With just enough of other people's blood cleaned off to make himself look halfway presentable, Harry went to his office in the Justice Building to make out his report on the night's events.

He had barely sat down and begun to work when the phone rang.

It was Mary Beth on the other end of the line. He could scarcely find the voice to speak to her, fearful of what news she might have for him.

"Harry, I just wanted you to know it looks like Drake'll be all right. The doctors say he's holding up nicely, and that if they can keep him free from infection he'll recover."

Harry smiled. The first heartening news he'd heard for a long while.

"He's right here if you want to speak to him."

"Yes, I do."

A moment passed as the receiver exchanged hands.

"Hello, Harry? How're you doing?" His voice sounded weak but not alarmingly so.

"I'm doing just fine, Drake. The important thing is how you're doing."

"Getting along. A little pain but I'm not complaining. I'm alive, ain't I?" He made an attempt at a laugh.

"That's right, you're alive, that's it."

"Tell me, Harry, how is our case coming along?"

"We got our man, Drake."

"You got Teddy?" Owens seemed immensely surprised.

"We certainly did. We got him good, Drake, we got him real good."